Strength From The Hills

Strength From The Hills

Jesse Stuart

Introduction By
JAMES M. GIFFORD

Edited By
JAMES M. GIFFORD
CHUCK D. CHARLES
ELEANOR G. KERSEY

Book Design By
PAMELA K. WISE

THE JESSE STUART FOUNDATION

Jesse Stuart Foundation
STRENGTH FROM THE HILLS

Copyright © 1960 by Jesse Stuart.
Copyright © 1988, by The Jesse Stuart Foundation.

All rights reserved. No part of this book may be reproduced or utilized in any form or by any means, electronic or mechanical, including photocopying, recording, or by any information storage or retrieval system, without permission in writing from the Publisher.

Library of Congress Cataloging-in-Publication Data

Stuart, Jesse, date
  [God's oddling]
  Strength from the hills : the story of Mick Stuart, my father : original title: God's oddling : the story of Mick Stuart, my father / edited by James M. Gifford, Chuck D. Charles, Eleanor Kersey.
    p. cm.
  Originally published: 1960.
  Summary: The author describes his father, a simple farmer who was rich in his love of living things and the strength he drew from the earth.
  ISBN 0-945984-29-3 : $12.00
  1. Stuart, Mick, 1880-1954- -Juvenile literature. 2. Stuart, Jesse, 1907-   - -Biography- -Family- -Juvenile literature.
  3. Authors, American- -20th century- -Biography- -Juvenile literature.
  4. Fathers and sons- -Kentucky- -Biography- -Juvenile literature.
  [1. Stuart, Mick, 1880-1954. 2. Farmers. 3. Mountain life.]
  I. Gifford, James M. II. Charles, Chuck D. III. Kersey, Eleanor.
  IV. Title.
PS3537.T92516Z464 1992
818'.5209- -dc20   92-3995
[B]   CIP
                                                                  AC

Published by:
The Jesse Stuart Foundation
P.O. Box 391
Ashland, KY 41114
1992

Dedicated to

KATHLEEN BEYER DORMAN
September 24, 1953
October 21, 1991

She gave me eyes, she gave me ears;
And humble cares, and delicate fears;
A heart, the fountain of sweet tears;
And love, and thought, and joy.

William Wordsworth

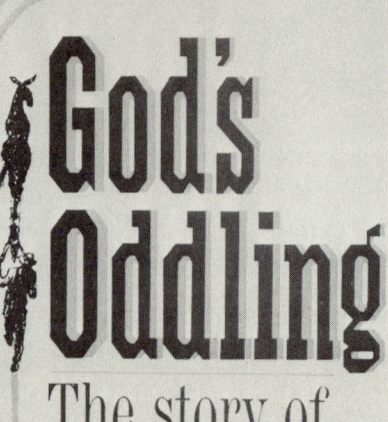

By James M. Gifford

Introduction

Several years ago, when the Kentucky Humanities Council began publishing their "New Books For New Readers" Series, I suggested that some "old books" might serve new readers, too. In particular, I recommended Jesse Stuart's Strength From The Hills.

Strength From The Hills: The Story of Mick Stuart, My Father, was originally published in 1968 by Pyramid Books of New York. It was an abridgement of God's Oddling, a full-length, 266 page biography of Mitchell Stuart, Jesse's father, that had been published by McGraw Hill in 1960. Strength From The Hills had been abbreviated to a 127 page book, and simplified for readers with a vocabulary at the 1000 word level, by Elinor Chamberlain. The primary purpose of this adaptation was to provide a book for adults who were learning English as a second language.

The Humanities Council did not have the funds to support a reprint of Strength From The Hills, so I kept the project on "the back burner," hoping to find a sponsor. Then, in the fall of 1991, at the Kentucky Book Fair in Frankfort, the First Lady, Mrs. Martha S. Wilkinson, introduced me to Mr. Thomas M. Dorman, the Governor's legislative liaison. Tom had recently suffered the tragic loss of his wife Kathy, who loved to read. Through Mrs. Wilkinson, she became an advocate for adult literacy programs in Kentucky.

With the generous promise that memorial gifts for Kathy Dorman would be applied to reprinting <u>Strength From The Hills</u>, my staff and I set out, in earnest, to edit this out-of-print book for republication. My colleagues and I discovered that much of the Kentucky flavor and language had been removed from the Chamberlain adaptation. In effect <u>God's Oddling had</u> been translated into a very mainstream book, and we had to do substantial editing in order to inject the original spirit of Stuart's powerful, evocative tribute to his father. The result is a book that will provide great benefit to adult new readers, who will thrill to Stuart's story of an earlier time in Kentucky's history, a time when people still lived off the land, much like their pioneer ancestors.

I want to acknowledge the bountiful aid and encouragement of many people. Chuck D. Charles and Eleanor G. Kersey played key roles in editing this book for republication. Bridget Chapman typed the text and made numerous corrections. Pamela K. Wise designed it and made it camera ready. Martha S. Wilkinson, Audrey Tayse Haynes, Executive Director of the Kentucky Literacy Commission, and Tom Dorman all provided enthusiastic support and encouragement.

Finally, in deep appreciation for her support of adult literacy programs, we are proud to dedicate this book to Kathy Dorman. Thanks to her husband Tom, and to her family and many friends, <u>Strength From The Hills</u> will become a monument to her life and work.

Table of Contents

Chapter 1	My Childhood	11
Chapter 2	War and Peace	25
Chapter 3	Family Life	35
Chapter 4	Father Buys A Farm	49
Chapter 5	A Good Neighbor	63
Chapter 6	"Bad To Drink"	77
Chapter 7	The Feud	87
Chapter 8	Uncle Jeff	97
Chapter 9	Home From College	105
Chapter 10	Men and Mules	117
Chapter 11	A Road To W-Hollow	123
Chapter 12	My Father's Wisdom	137
Chapter 13	Father Was Not Afraid To Die	151
Chapter 14	I Think I Hear His Footsteps	165

*The cabin where Jesse Stuart was born.
Photo by Earl Palmer.*

Chapter 1

My Childhood

I was born in the high hills of Kentucky. The log house where I was born had one room. It was five miles from the town of Riverton, Kentucky, where there was a post office.

My birth place, Cedar Riffles, was lonely. The Little Sandy River was near, and we could hear the waters on quiet nights.

When we lived there, we could hear foxes barking from the lonely hilltops. Squirrels played in the tall trees near our home. Rabbits played around the house and went into the garden to eat our plants. We often saw snakes near the house.

We had only one book in our house. That was the Holy Bible. We kept it on a little table, where everyone could see it.

Above the Bible, hanging on the wall, was our shotgun. It was ready for my father to use to protect the family or livestock.

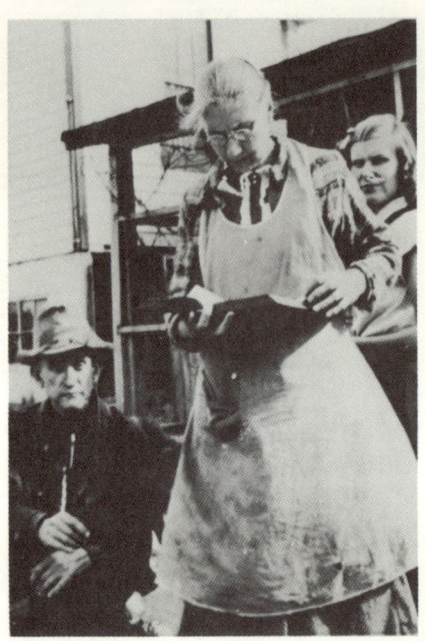

We had only one book in our house...the Holy Bible.

"We always had good dogs on the farm."

We did not own the one-room house. We rented it.

We always had good dogs on the farm. We began training them to hunt foxes when they were young. There were always wild animals in the weeds near by. We used them to teach our dogs to hunt and kill.

In the wild life of the high hills, every animal was waiting to eat another animal.

Wild dogs killed sheep and cattle. Buzzards and crows flying above were waiting for their share of the meat. Foxes killed birds, chickens, and rabbits. Our dogs learned to kill the wild dogs, the foxes, and snakes.

Man was the great enemy of wild animals. He killed to save his livestock. He killed for food.

My father worked in the coal mines during the winter. He left home before daylight and returned after dark. When he returned, his old clothes were always thick with mud. It was not easy to wash the mud off his hands.

During the summer, he farmed the hillsides. He had no other land to farm. He used mules for farm work. They were better than horses on the hillsides.

We grew corn and tobacco. We did not work much with the corn. It grew fast in the new soil. It usually grew well, except in very dry weather.

But the tobacco fields! I can never forget long tobacco rows on a hillside with the hot sun shining down. I can still feel the hot dry soil under my feet and hear the sound of the hoes as men and women cut down the weeds.

In March, we sowed the tobacco seed beds. Later in the Spring, we moved the young plants to the fields.

We worked in the tobacco fields all summer long. Before winter came, we cut the tobacco. Then we prepared it for market. When it was ready, we took it to market.

We often took it twenty miles. We sold it for three, four, five, or nine cents per pound. The best only brought ten cents per pound.

Tobacco brings money to farmers in the Eastern Kentucky hills.

My father worked hard every day but he always took time to hunt. Hunting was fun for him. All the Stuarts loved guns. They loved to carry them.

He often hunted from morning until night. When I was big enough, I went with him. When he had killed all the rabbits that I could carry, he laughed. That was my job, to carry them.

"Men from cities do not know how to hunt," he said. "They have fine guns, hunting coats, and special dogs. But I can take my dog and my old gun and do better than they do."

Jesse Stuart and his brother James. "All the Stuarts loved guns. They loved to carry them."

One winter we left Cedar Riffles for a new home. Snow lay on the ground. Snowbirds were flying among the trees along the roadside.

My father was driving a yoke of oxen. They were stronger than horses or mules. They pulled a sled, which carried most of our belongings.

My mother was driving a horse that pulled another sled. My sister sat beside me on the seat next to my mother. A lap robe covered our legs. The snow hit our faces. The wind went through our clothes, but we did not seem to feel it. We were used to being cold.

We were going to a log house in W-Hollow. The hollow was a valley with a stream at the bottom. The stream was in the shape of the letter W. And our place was at the top and middle of the W with trees all around it.

"We must cut down the trees," my father said. "We must start a new place. Then we must leave it for other people." That is what we always did. We made a farm and then moved on.

When I was six, I learned to use an ax and a hoe. When I was eleven, I learned to plow. There were no holidays for children on Kentucky's tree-covered hillside farms.

Father had to pay 12 dollars every month to rent the 100 acre farm. He would not pay more when the rent went up. Again we had to find a new home.

But we were glad to go. We could see another house from where we lived. We did not like to live so near to other people. "This place is almost like a town," my mother said.

Our family had grown. It had three new children while we were living there. It had lost one.

It was the middle of winter when we were preparing to move. Herbert suddenly became sick with pneumonia and died. I remember my father's sadness. I remember hearing him say, "If we could have had a doctor here, we might have saved him!"

I remember the wagon with the plain wood box on it. Two mules pulled it. I remember the wagons that followed. We went five miles to my grandfather's farm to bury Herbert.

My grandfather was there. His white hair was waving in the wind. He called to the driver, "Come this way." The wagons went across a little field and then to the top of a hill.

I remember the songs. I remember some of the words. I remember how cold my feet were, standing in the mud. I remember how people cried.

All the others in the family cried, but I did not. I cried when I returned home and Herbert was gone.

That night at the fireside Mother said: "I feel free to leave here now. Herbert is buried on land that belongs to my father. He will not sell it. You know that I could not leave here and leave my son's grave. We do not own any land for his grave. But I can rest tonight."

"We must go now. I cannot live in this place any longer."

I wanted another brother. I often said to Mother: "I want another brother. Herbert is not here. I have no brother to play with. I have no brother to help me gather eggs. I have no brother to walk in the stream with me."

I remember how my mother cried. She did not speak. She sat there, making our clothes. She often helped the neighbor women make clothes. She often helped when there was sickness in their homes. They came to her for help.

I remember going into the forest and listening to the wind. I was looking for my brother Herbert. I did not understand why he was gone. I could hear him in the wind. I called to him.

But no answer. Only the wind. Life was strange. I could not understand how the earth could hold Herbert and let me live.

I said to Mother: "Why did Herbert die? Why does any person die? Why don't we live forever?"

And Mother said: "It is God's plan, son. We are like the flowers. We come for a season, like them. They come at the beginning of summer. At the end of the summer they die."

And then I said: "God is not fair. Herbert sleeps under the ground, Mom. You know how hard that bed is. I want Herbert to play with me. I do not like to play with my sisters."

I remember how she cried.

I was the only boy in W-Hollow then. I did not like to play with girls.

One day I saw a man riding toward our house. He had a big horse. Its legs were covered with mud. He carried a little bag.

I ran to the house. We did not often see a man pass our house.

The stranger met me at the door. He patted my head. He asked me to hug his neck. He said: "You will do it when you see what I have brought you."

I ran into the house. I heard a small voice. I said: "Is it another Herbert? Is it, Mom?"

She was there in bed. She smiled. She pulled the cover away. I saw the baby. "Here is your brother that the doctor brought you," said Mother.

"Where did he get him?" I said.

"From behind an old tree on the hill."

I ran to the hill. I looked behind every tree. It was strange that I had found many eggs there and had never found a baby. I ran wildly, looking for another baby. I ran to the house and told Mother that I could find no babies.

Mother said: "Only doctors can find babies."

That night Father said: "I want to name this boy James. It is a name I like. I have a brother named James. Four of my brothers have sons named James. I must have a James."

Mother said: "Add Mitchell to it. That is your name, the name of your father, your father's father, and your father's father's father.

And I had a brother James Mitchell.

Mother often said: "I do not want to live here any more, Mick. Herbert died in this house. We must go to another place. I think I can hear Herbert walking when the wind blows. He is with me here."

Father said: "As soon as another family leaves a house in the Hollow, we will get it."

Then there was a house. Father rented it.

He found work for himself for a dollar and 25 cents a day. He found work for me for 25 cents per day. Mother got work for 25 cents a day.

"We need the money," Father said. "I have not yet paid for Herbert's casket. It cost 15 dollars. I will pay what I owe."

A wagon carried our chairs and tables and beds. It was the same wagon that had carried Herbert to his grave. I led the cows. I called the dogs, and I returned to get the chickens.

I had never seen a place as bad and lonely as our new place. My father was sick there. Our corn died in the ground, because the ground never became warm and dry. The fruit was killed that year by the cold. The cows were sick.

But we did not lose hope. My mother would never lose hope.

My mother made jelly from wild grapes.

I cut young trees, and then I cut the wood into thin strips. My mother made baskets with them, and I sold the baskets. She told me to say that my father had made them.

They were strong baskets. I saw one, years later, when I had finished college. I thought of a bad winter and a woman's hand when I saw it. As she labored on baskets, my mother said: "This is going to be a bad winter."

That was the winter of 1917. Snow lay on the ground during the whole winter. Hundreds of birds died. Rabbits were only skin and bones. Cows became thin.

The forest grew close to our house. Owls hooted from the dark trees in the middle of the day. We found a snake in the house. Father killed it. I remember the dark blood on the floor.

Mother said: "This is a God-forsaken place. I can't live here."

We could hear the owls carry away our chickens at night. Father often ran out in the snow with nothing on his feet. We could hear the foxes bark from hills above the house. We could hear the wind break branches from the trees.

James was four years old. He took the dogs to the cornfields. At four years old, he tried to hunt.

I hunted with my father at night. I carried the

animals he killed. We ate their meat and sold their skins.

We gathered roots and herbs to make medicine. We sold them.

We picked wild strawberries, raspberries, and blackberries and sold them. We sold them at the houses in town, which was named Greenup.

We got enough money for food and for winter clothes. We paid for Herbert's coffin. I worked from before sunup until after sundown for my 25 cents.

Father said: "You must have book-learning, son. You must not grow up like me. I can not write my name."

I walked three miles with my sister to school. We met foxes in our path many mornings. Squirrels played over our heads in the tall trees. Some jumped across the road in front of us.

We met other children. I wanted to learn more than the other boys. When I did better, I laughed. When another did better, I cried.

I loved school. I learned fast, because I tried to learn.

My sister learned fast. People said: "Sal Stuart's children learn fast. They fight like wild animals. The girl is always clean and pretty. The boy's hands are hard and never clean."

One day at the end of winter, Sophia called me to the house. I heard a baby's voice. It was a weak voice. I was sure that I did not have another brother.

"Another brother," said Mother. "But he is very little." She named him Lee.

He was not strong enough to live long. The same wagon that had carried Herbert carried Lee away. He was buried beside Herbert.

A heavy snow fell very late that year, after winter had ended. My father and I were walking to the barn where we kept the cows and mules. In deep snow, I always stepped where he had stepped. This time I did not.

I said to myself: "Dad, you were born among the hills. You will die among them. You have let them hold you. You will lie forever beside my brothers. Life should have been better for them. Why didn't you make life better for them? These dark hills will not always hold me. I shall go beyond them some day."

Again my mother said: "I can't live here any more." We had cleared this farm. We had made new fences. We had again prepared a place where other people would live. My father rented another house in W-Hollow. It was a log house on a hillside. There were flowers around it. But we had no time for flowers.

Jesse's mother, Martha Hylton Stuart, when she was very young.

Chapter 2

War and Peace

Life was hard for my mother. Before my brother Herbert died, there was a time when she felt that she could not continue with our hard life.

This is how I remember it.

"I can't do it any more, Mick," Mother said. "I am leaving you. I am going home to my father. He will give me and my children the best that he has." "We are different people," said Father. "I am sorry about everything, Sal. If I say things that hurt you, I am sorry."

"Since we are not happy together," Mother said, "it is better to part now. It is better to part before we have more children." My brother Herbert was ready for the trip. He was dressed in a white dress. He was lying in bed playing with a spinning top. Mother gave him the top so that he would be quiet while she dressed me. "He has the top that Dad made for me," I said. "I do not want him to have it. I want to take it with me."

My father moved in his chair. He crossed his legs. He was smoking his pipe. He blew small clouds of tobacco smoke into the room.

"You are taking all the children and leaving me alone!" he said.

"They are mine," said Mother. "I will have all three, or fight every one in W-Hollow."

"If you let Sophia stay," said Father, "she will soon be old enough to cook for me. I do not like to eat the food I cook."

"You should have no better, Mick," said Mother.

"I should have better," said Father. "I will stay here and make a good farm. And you will return, Sal."

"That may be what you expect," Mother said with anger. "But I will not return. I never want to see this house again."

"It is the best house I can give you," Father said.

"I am not thinking about the house," Mother said. "Mick, it is you. Your mind changes more than the weather. I never know what to expect."

"We are not the same people," Father said. "That is why I love you, Sal. You are not like I am. You are as solid as a mountain oak. I need you, Sal. I need you more than any person in this world."

"I am leaving!" Mother said. "I have had enough of this. I have wanted to go before. But I felt sorry for you. I felt sorry for my little children without a father. This is the third time I have been ready to go. The third time is the charm. I am going."

"I am ready, Mom." said Sophia. She was dressed in a blue dress. Her yellow hair fell over her shoulders.

Father turned slowly and looked at Sophia. He blew a cloud of smoke slowly from his mouth. "Listen," he said. "It will rain soon. I hear thunder."

"I do not hear anything," said Mother.

Father rose from his chair. He walked to the door. "The rains come over the mountain to our right," he said. "I have seen them come often. But the sky is blue—except for one long thin cloud, like a horse's tail. That means that there will be rain within three days."

"We have five miles to walk," said Mother. "We will be at my father's house in three hours."

"Listen," said Father. "I can hear it. I have good ears."

"I do not hear it," said Mother.

"You will hear it soon," said Father. "It is like wagons rolling across the far sky."

"Third time is the right time for me," said Mother.

"See the birds," said Father. "Look out there, Sal! They are hurrying home. That means that a storm is coming."

She looked outside.

"Listen, Sal—listen—"

"Yes, Mick. I hear it."

"Will we go?" Sophia asked.

"Yes, we will go before the storm."

"But it is coming fast, Sal. Will you take our children out in a storm? The birds know more than you do."

She turned from the front door without speaking. She walked across the room. She took clothes and put them carefully on a chair. She looked at the chair.

I knew what she was thinking. She remembered when the chair seats were broken. She remembered when Father promised to make new seats. She remembered when Father stopped plowing one day and made new seats for the chairs.

Father was smoking again. I never saw him smoke so much or blow such clouds of smoke from his mouth.

"The sun is gone from the sky, Sal," he said. He was watching her face as he spoke. "There is a black cloud racing over the sky as fast as a hound dog chasing a fox."

She did not hear him. She was moving clothes.

"Bring me the basket, Jesse," she said.

I got the big basket. It was the egg basket. When I gathered eggs, I put them in this basket.

"Where will Dad put the eggs?" I asked.

The lonely hilltops of W-Hollow.
Photo by Earl Palmer.

"Forget that, Jesse," she said. "We will let him find a place to put eggs."

She put our clothes into the big basket. I saw her looking at the basket which Dad had made when Sophia was a baby. Every week Mother and Father went to town with this basket filled with eggs. At the stores they traded the eggs for salt, sugar, cloth, and other things that they needed.

"Listen to the rain, Sal," Father said. "Hear it hitting the house!"

Mother had our clothes in the big basket. She walked to the door. The rain was rushing down from the top of the house into the big water barrel.

"You cannot wash my hair in rain water any more," Sophia said. "Will my hair still be curly?"

"I do not know," said Mother.

"You said that other water would be bad for my hair," Sophia said.

"Mom can use any water for my hair," I said.

Mother walked across the room. She looked out at the rocks on the mountainside. I knew that she remembered helping Dad there. She held a light for him on dark winter nights, when he brought baby lambs to the house, to warm them in front of the fireplace.

She looked at the white flowers near those rocks. I knew what she was thinking. "Mick brought flowers for me many evenings after plowing all day. Yes, bad as he is to cuss, Mick loves a wild flower."

Mother walked into the big kitchen.

"Are we going?" I asked as I followed her.

"It is raining," Mother answered. "You know that we are not going."

"If we go, who will cook for Dad?" Mother did

not answer. She looked at the window box that Father made for her. He filled it with black soil. He made it for her flower seeds. He put it in the kitchen window, where it would catch the early morning sunlight.

"My little basket is ready," Sophia said. She came running to Mother.

"I am ready, too. I will take my playthings. You know that Dad won't play with them. He plays with the mules. He says that they are his playthings."

"Yes," Mother said, "your father—"

The sky was low. The rain fell in steady streams. The trees, the plants, the flowers, drank the rain. The rain washed them clean just as Mother washed my face, hands, neck, and ears.

It had never rained this hard before.

"It is a bad storm, Sal," Father said as he walked into the kitchen. "If you had taken little Herbert on the long road to your father's place—"

"Do not talk about the road," said Mother.

"Where is my top?" I asked.

"Herbert is asleep with it in his hand," Father answered.

"When we go, I will take it with me."

Cool air from the rain blew through the house.

"The rain has chilled the air so," said Father, "that a person needs a coat."

Through the rain-washed windows, Mother looked

at the garden. She saw the little bench that Father made. Mother and Father sat together on it. They cleaned beans and shucked corn for cooking. They sat there during the long summer evenings when the crickets sang in the garden. Father smoked his pipe, and Mother smoked her pipe. We played near them.

"The sun, Mom," I said. "Look—we can go now."

Father looked at the red ball of sun hanging brightly in the blue sky above the mountain. His brown, weather-beaten face became sad.

"This is the third time," said Mother, "when I have been ready to go. Something has happened every time. I am not going."

"We are not going?" Sophia asked.

"No, we are not going."

"What will I do with my basket of playthings?"

"Put them where you got them."

Father smiled. He was happy.

"Come, Sal," said Father. "We will see if our sweet potatoes have begun to grow."

They walked from the kitchen to the garden. Father had his arm around Mother. "I think the potatoes have begun to sprout," I heard him say.

I went to see if Herbert had my top in his hand. It was mine, because Father made it for me.

Between high hills, my Love, we have our shack,
A growing garden, hives for honeybees;
We have our cattle, barn and bins and stack,
And we have blooming flowers and shrubs and trees.
We have steep mountain slopes of growing grain,
Tobacco, corn, potatoes, cane and wheat;
Our loamy land will yield if we get rain . . .
Should we have drouth, we must expect defeat.
We'll pick wild huckleberries from the ridges,
And wild blackberries from the dogwood's shade,
And wild strawberries from the south-hill ledges
To can and store before our crops are made.
We must be ready when this season passes
With cans of fruit, with bulging barn and bins,
With sorghum made, with bright full jelly glasses
To face the coming snows and icy winds.

Jesse Stuart

The Stuart family, L to R, Glennis, James, Mary, Jesse, Sophie, Martha, and Mitchell.

Chapter 3

Family Life

When I was a child, a bell called us to eat at the end of the day. This was the best time of the day for all of us. We stopped what we were doing and hurried to the house.

This was the time when each member of the family told what he had done that day. We sometimes sat around the table talking and planning for three hours after we finished eating.

My father talked about his father and his brothers and sisters. My father was the youngest of 11 children. All the boys, and girls, too, worked in the fields.

Mother told us stories of her father and his great strength.

In those days people had few books and no newspapers to read in the Kentucky hills, so people told the same stories again and again for entertainment.

I liked these stories. I never wanted them to come to an end. It was never easy for me to wait until we finished eating. I wanted to hear our parents talk of long ago.

After my sister and I began school, we had something to talk about, too. Our father and mother were good listeners.

One of my father's pleasures was to talk about other farms. He talked about a different farm each evening. He told us what he would do with it, if he could buy it. He told us where he would plant fruit trees. He told us where he would build a home.

When he finished, the farms were much better. They were beautiful. We felt that we owned them.

We went to the table hungry. We came away happy, full of food and great dreams.

When we went to live on our seventh rented farm, we did not have much food on our table. The soil was not good. It would not produce much. A sister was born there. Now my father had a family of seven to feed.

We did not have much to eat, but we enjoyed sitting at the table.

For months of the year, we were completely separated from the world by deep snow. We lived in our own world with our own thoughts. We had no roads. When it snowed, we were alone.

There was not a winter road in W-Hollow until after World War II. But we had a car, so we tried to build a road. We also built bridges. The road was often full of mudholes.

We looked at the sky and studied the weather before we started the car. The weather often surprised us.

Today we have a good winter road. We can go to Greenup in less than ten minutes. In the old days there was deep mud in the roads. We used horses and a wagon. I needed a half day to go to Greenup. I could not always return the same day.

My father always tried to guess what the weather would be. He had many rules to help him guess.

He said that a circle around the moon meant bad weather within three days. A very bright circle meant bad weather within a week.

Sometimes we could hear a steam boat whistle carried by the wind from the Ohio River, six miles away. We prepared then for a long period of bad weather. We hurried to Greenup for necessary supplies. We went on horseback, or we walked.

Red sky in the morning brought bad weather, too. And there were other things that told that a storm was coming.

These were some of our rules about the weather. They were not always true, but we enjoyed using these rules.

My father loved the land and everything on it. He

liked to see things grow. As soon as he could lead me by the hand, I went with him everywhere on the farm. When I could walk no more, he carried me. I learned to love many of the things he loved.

I went with him to many fields. I listened to him talk about their beauty. I know now that he had wonderful thoughts which should have been put in writing.

Long ago, my father put me down under some trees. "Look at this hill, son," he said. "Look up this hill toward the sky. See how pretty that new corn is."

That was the first field that I remember. The rows of dark-green corn followed the high hillside. I could hear the wind in the corn. My father said that the corn was talking and he could understand what the corn was saying.

I went down on my knees to look at the corn. "This corn has no mouth," I told him. "How can anything talk without a mouth?"

He laughed and we went away from the field. One day he took me across two valleys to see some corn. He had cut the trees on this land. He had planted white corn, to make our bread. He thought that this was a good place for white corn. Someone had brought the seed from the Big Sandy River valley. My father had lived near the Big Sandy River until he was 16 years old.

My father said that he could understand what the corn was saying.

Among the corn, he had planted beans. He had also planted pumpkins. There were fruits of many different colors—yellow, white, green, brown. These plants delighted him.

"Look at this corn," my father said. "Look at these beans, these pumpkins! I could walk across this field, stepping on pumpkins, never stepping on the ground."

He loved the beauty of fields and plants. He did not often think of his fields for the money they would bring. He knew the value of a dollar, but money did not mean everything to him. He liked to see the beauty of growing things.

One rainy day, he pointed to a redbird in a tree. "Did you ever see anything as pretty as that redbird with the raindrops on her?" Since that day, I have liked to see birds, especially redbirds, sitting in the rain. My father showed me the beauty.

"A blacksnake is a pretty thing," he said to me. I never before heard a man say that a snake is pretty. I always remember him saying it. I remember the place where we saw the snake.

No other man saw so much beauty in trees. When he walked through the forest, he laid his hand upon the trees. He said that this tree or that tree was beautiful. Then he pointed to other trees and said that they should be cut down. He always told his reasons.

Hundreds of times he took me to the hills to see

wild flowers. I did not understand at first. He sat on a log, looking at some flowers. When the sun went down, we went home.

Sometimes, going to a field to work, he stopped the horse beside a stream. He sat and looked at the water. He watched the small fish in a deep hole. He did not say a word.

I kept quiet, too. I looked around, wondering why he had stopped. But I never asked him. Sometimes he told me why, and sometimes he did not.

Then he went to the field. Then he worked very fast, because he had lost time.

My father did not need to travel to see something beautiful. He found beauty everywhere. He had eyes to find it. He had a mind to know it. He had a heart to feel it.

He went to feed the horses and mules at four in the morning, when the stars were bright. In winter, there might be snow on the ground. He put the corn in the feedboxes, and then went outside to look at the morning moon. He always had a horse with a yellow mane and tail. He liked to see such a horse run in the moonlight.

He often took me to see a new tree, or a pretty plant. He found many strange and beautiful things. I also tried to discover strange and beautiful things.

Many people thought that my father was only a

Mick Stuart's horses, Doc and Bess.
Photo by Mahan of Ashland.

poor farmer. They saw only a little man, in clean but old clothes. They saw his hard hands. They saw him in a field, looking at something. They thought that he was looking into space, thinking of nothing.

But he was looking at a flower, or a plant, or a new bug. Or he was looking at the beauty in a tree.

Those who truly knew him were never sorry for him. They wished to be like him. My father had his own world. It was larger and richer than the whole earth is to other men. But he could not write the words to express his thoughts.

When I was three years old, my father carried me three miles to see a schoolhouse. He carried me on his back. He told me that he was the horse and I was the rider.

The building was painted white. He lifted me from his back to the ground. It was the first schoolground that I ever put my feet on.

"I wanted this schoolhouse for you, son," he said. "I never went to school. I do not want my young-ones to grow up without going to school. If I could only read and write!"

Though my father could not read or write he served as a school trustee for the Plum Grove District. I do not believe that a man with a good education could have done better. He left his corn in weeds to go over the district getting the people to petition for the new schoolhouse.

He had cut down the trees on the schoolground. He had helped with the building. He did everything he could for the Plum Grove school.

From the first days that I remember, Father talked to me about going to school. During winter evenings, he talked about learning to read and write. When I was riding behind him on the mule, he talked about reading and writing.

He made me a small wooden plow. He was plowing around a mountainside. I tried to follow him, plowing with my little plow. But soon I was far behind him.

"The rows are long," I said.

"These rows are short," he answered, laughing.

But the rows around this mountainside were long to me. They were long for the mule, too. Father was not yet 30 years old, and he was very strong.

That evening he talked to me about going to school. "The man who plows will have food to eat," he said. "That is as sure as anything can be sure. But I want you to learn to read, write, and understand numbers. I want that more than anything else in this world."

At the age of five, I started to the new schoolhouse at Plum Grove. Every afternoon Father asked what I was learning. He was pleased because I liked to go to school.

"I can do something that you can't do," I said to him. It was before the end of my first year in school.

"What is that, son?" he asked me.

"I can read and write my name."

My father sat looking at the fire. I did not know then that I had hurt him. I know now that I did.

I wanted to be the best student in my school. I studied. I read every book I could find. In each year at school, I finished two years of work.

My father wanted me to go to school. But we needed money. Our corn had failed for two years. I had to quit school to work for another farmer for 25 cents a day. My father and his big horse Fred worked for two dollars a day. My mother worked for 25 cents a day.

I remember well the first time I cut corn with my father. I was nine years old, but I was tall and strong. The sun was rising as I followed my father under the trees.

"I tell you, son," Father told me, "there is nothing in the world better than this. Nothing is better than cutting corn on an early morning. This is the best time of the year. I want you to know the beauty of it."

We came to an open space on the far side of the forest. We had arrived at the cornfield. It was on the side of a mountain. In Eastern Kentucky, cornfields are often found on mountainsides.

I stood beside my father on the mountaintop. We looked down the mountain at the great field of corn. A 30 acre cornfield spread over that mountainside. That is a big field of corn.

"Here is where I will teach you to cut corn," Father said. "It seems like a lot of work, when you look at it like this. But it is not. Cutting corn is fast work, if you know how. We will go down, and cut up the mountain!"

At the bottom my father stood for a minute, looking up. "There is not a job on the farm that I would rather do," he said. "It is pretty work. Look at this field. I wonder what the corn is talking about. Do you hear it talking?"

He covered his neck with a big blue bandanna.

"Do like this," he said. "When the sun comes over the mountain and dries the corn, it will burn your neck. But if you cover your neck, it won't."

I also tied a bandanna around my neck.

"We are ready, son." he said. "You watch me. First, we count." He counted six rows.

He showed me how to plan our work. He showed me how to tie four of the corn plants together without cutting them. These made a strong center to which we could tie the cut plants. The centers, called riders, would help the cut plants to stand firmly in the field. They would remain here until they were brown and dry.

"It is always best to tie a row of riders first," he said. "Then come through the field again and cut corn and put it around the riders. I will show you how."

Cutting corn was not easy for me. But I liked it. I liked looking behind me, to see what I had done. I was doing something important. My father was famous as a corn cutter, and he was teaching me how to do it.

"I love this work," I told Father.

"I told you that cutting corn is like play," he said.

I worked a week there with my father. Since I was six, he had been teaching me that working with my hands was honorable. I had never liked some of the work. But I enjoyed cutting corn.

I went to bed hoping the night would soon pass. I wanted to return to the big cornfield.

After one week's work, we had finished cutting our field of corn. We counted the riders with the cut corn tied around them. There were 455, standing straight and pretty and tied well at the tops.

"Next week we will cut your Uncle Mel's corn," Father said. "When we finish that, we will cut Bill Duncan's. Others have asked me to cut their corn. We can do it, son! We can do it together! You are a real corn cutter."

We looked down the mountain at the great field of corn.

Jesse's sister, Sophie.

Chapter 4

Father Buys A Farm

When I was a child, we never had enough money to buy land. "We should buy land, Mick," Mother said. "If we do not, we lose things."

"We should find a piece of land without a house on it. We could pay for that more easily. We can build a house."

"There is only one possible place in W-Hollow," Father said. "It is 50 acres. No one else wants it. There is not a fence on it. There is not a building on it. I can buy it for six dollars per acre."

"It is good land. There are several little streams. But three hundred dollars is a lot of money."

"But we can buy it." Mother said. "We can sell two cows and make the first payment. I think about the two boys in their graves on my father's farm. I want a place for graves."

"I can buy this place," Father said. We had looked at every acre. "It has enough good water. It has everything I want. Only one thing is wrong. Do you know what it is?"

"There is not a building on it," I said. "It is covered with trees."

We had looked at it carefully. We had made deep holes in the ground. Father had let the soil pass through his fingers. We had been on the hilltops and down in the valleys.

"We can cut the trees," he said. "We can build a house. That is not what is wrong. But there is not a wagon road leading to this farm."

The place had once belonged to Jack Sinnett. "How did the Sinnetts travel when they lived here?" I asked.

"There is an old road," he said. "But that was 50 years ago. Trees grow in the road now. There are fences across it."

"Then you won't buy this farm?" I said.

"Yes, I will buy it," he replied quickly. "Any place I buy will have something wrong. If it did not, it would cost more money. We will buy it and then do something about the road."

He made the first payment, using the two cows. We had two other cows and would soon have two more.

At the end of the winter, in 1920, we went to live on Uncle Martin Hilton's farm. It was beside our 50 acres.

"I will build a house as soon as I can," my father

said. "But first I will build a barn for our livestock."

"There is a house on my land, Mitch," Uncle Martin Hilton said. "I do not use it. I will give it to you for a barn, if you will move it."

We moved it. We carried the logs to our land. The men came from neighboring farms and helped build the walls again.

"Now we must build a house," Father said. The place where we planned to build our home was covered with trees. Some were so close together that a man could pass through only on his hands and knees.

First, we cleared a place for a garden. Then we cleared ground for corn and tobacco.

My father made a very pretty little farm. It was as pretty as any farm in our part of Kentucky. He never hurt his land. He cared for it like a living thing.

He planted our corn in the dark of the moon, so it would grow tall and produce more corn.

He planted our potatoes in the light of the moon, so they would not grow very deep in the ground.

Perhaps it was not wise to believe this. But plants grew well for him, although the soil was thin.

"We have everything planted, son," Father said. "You, Sophia, and Sal must care for it. I must find work so that I can pay for the land."

He got a job on the railroad. It was the best job that he ever had. This was in 1921, and I was 14 years old. My grandfather, Nathan Hilton, had come to live with us. He was 75 years old.

Grandfather and I planned to build the house while Father worked on the railroad.

"We can pay for the land, build a house, and make a road," Father said one evening. We were at the table eating. He had walked five miles across the mountain, after working ten hours on the railroad. His pay for the day's work was two dollars and 84 cents.

At the end of the winter, in 1921, Grandfather and I started building our house. We cut trees and made logs for the walls. We cut some logs into small, thin pieces, to make shingles for the roof.

At the end of the summer, we had a "house-raising." We asked all the neighbors to come. The men came to help with the house. The women came to help Mother cook. I remember that 29 men came. I remember the big table filled with good food.

But Grandfather and I were the real builders of the house. I remember how we worked. Grandfather was a powerful man, with broad shoulders. He weighed 220 pounds.

We began living in the house before it was finished. A short time before that, my mother gave birth to her seventh child, Glennis Juanita.

One of our neighbors allowed us to move our furniture and household goods across his land. But he said that we could never drive a wagon across his land again.

My father said, "I expect to remain on this farm. It is my own land. I shall have a fine farm here some day."

This is the place where the Stuarts still live today.

It was better to work on our own land. My father said, "I have used my strength on other men's land. Now I am old and I have my own land."

It was home. And it was good to have a home. It was a lonely place. But it was home. It was good to have a piece of land where we could bury dead. It was good to hear the birds returning at the end of each winter. It was good to see the flowers at the front door.

We had been living on our farm only a short while when Jake Timmins came.

We were working in the barn. We watched him walk toward us. He was a small man, with a beard.

"Hello, Mick," Jake said. He looked at the barn.

"Hello, Jake," Father said. We had heard that Jake Timmins took farms away from other men. Father was afraid. I saw that his hands were shaking.

"I see that you are doing more work on this barn," Jake said.

"I want it ready for winter," Father told him.

"Stop now, Mick," Jake said. "I do not want you to work for me and get no pay for it."

"What do you mean, Jake?" Father asked.

"You have put your barn on my land, Mick," he said with a little laugh. "This is my land. I do not want to take it, with this fine barn on it, but it is mine and I must take it."

"It is not your land, Jake," Father said. "I have lived near here since I was a boy. I know where my land ends. Those rocks with that row of trees mark the edge of my land!"

"No. You are wrong," Jake said. "One corner of your land is at that big dead tree. Another corner is there at the top of that hill."

"That includes ten acres of my best land," Father said. "It includes this barn. It includes my garden. It almost includes my house!"

My father's lips were shaking while he spoke.

"Tim Mennix sold you land that belongs to me," Jake said.

"You should have said something before I built on it," Father said.

"Sorry, Mick," Jake said, "but I must go now. I have told you. You are building on my land!"

"This land is mine!" Father told him. "I gave my money for it. I expect to keep it."

"Do not destroy this barn," Jake told Father as he turned to walk away. "It belongs to me!"

"I will not destroy this barn, Jake," Father said. "I expect to feed my cows and mules in it this winter!"

Father and I watched him. He stopped and looked at the barn. He looked at our garden with the new fence around it. He looked at the new house.

"He will say that the house, too, is his," Father said. "I will talk to Tim Mennix."

I went with him. We hurried along the mountainside. Tim lived two miles away. He was cutting wood near his house.

"Jake Timmins is trying to take my land," Father told Tim. "He says it was not your land to sell."

"Those rocks with that row of trees mark the edge of the piece of land," Tim said. "They have marked the edge for 70 years. But when Jake Timmins wants a piece of land, he takes it."

"People have told me that," Father said. "People said that he would take my land if I lived beside him ten years."

"He will take it before ten years, Mick," Tim Mennix said. His voice was shaking. "He had only one acre at the beginning. That acre was where three farms joined together. The acre had no value. None of the farmers wanted it. They had built no fences. He took it."

"Then he began building fences on other people's farms. They asked a judge to decide who was right. And every time, Jake got the land. That has happened 40 times."

"I will ask Finn Madden to measure my land," Father said. "He is the county surveyor. His job is measuring land. He will do it lawfully."

"That will not help you," Tim told Father. "Finn Madden is a good friend to Jake Timmins."

"But I must have Finn Madden," Father said. "He is the only man who can do it lawfully."

"Be careful," Tim Mennix said. "Jake Timmins is a bad man."

"I have heard that," Father said. "I do not want any trouble. I am a married man with a family."

When we returned home, we saw Jake on one little hill, measuring the land toward another little hill. He walked toward the other hill, putting pieces of wood in the ground to mark where he measured. One piece of wood was about five feet from the corner of our house.

Father started to go to meet him, but Mother stopped him. She said that we must let the law decide.

And that night Father could not sleep. I heard him walking across the room again and again.

Jake was the most feared man among our hills.

He had started with one acre and now had more than 400 acres. He had taken them all from other people.

The next day Finn Madden came with Jake. Together they marked the edge of the land. It was the same as Jake had already marked.

When they finished, Finn Madden told Father, "Tim Mennix sold you land that was not his. You are losing the best part of your land, Mick."

"What are you planning to do, Dad?" I asked.

He did not answer. He watched the two men as they walked away.

"Mother wants no one hurt because of land," I said.

"But this is my land," Father said.

The next day the sheriff came. He gave several orders. Father must take his cows and mules out of the barn that we had built for them. Our chickens must not go into the garden. We must not walk on a part of the land near our house.

"He will take the house too if we do not stop him," Father said. He thought and thought about what to do. Then he dressed in his best clothes.

"I will go to Uncle Mel," he said. "He has been in many fights about fences. He can tell me what to do."

While Father was gone, Jake Timmins brought winter food for his cows to the barn that we had built.

When Father returned, Uncle Mel came with him.

Uncle Mel carried a big ax across his shoulder. Before they arrived at the house, Father showed Uncle Mel the land Jake Timmins had taken.

"Men like him are as bad as snakes," Uncle Mel said. Uncle Mel was 82 years old, but his eyes were good and his shoulders were broad and his hands were big and strong. He had been cutting down trees all his life. "He can't do this to you, Mick!"

Uncle Mel's anger was more than Father's when he looked at the land. "Any one would know where the edge of your land is. It must follow those rocks," Uncle Mel said. "He is taking your land. I will help you get it again."

That night Father and Uncle Mel studied Father's deed. This was the paper that belonged to the owner of the land. It proved that the land had lawfully been sold to Father. It told the size and shape of the land, with all the measurements.

Uncle Mel could not read very well. I helped him. "We must get another paper," Uncle Mel said. "We must do this according to law. We must get a court order telling me to find the edge of your land. And then I will find it."

I did not know, then, why he wanted this second paper. But I learned why. Without it, he could not cut into any trees marking the measurements.

When he had this paper, he began. He and Father

Uncle Marion Stewart and his wife, Mary Ann, who was Mitchell Stuart's sister. Uncle Marion was Uncle Mel in Jesse's writings.

Jesse and his baby sister, Glennis.

had asked some neighbors to come and watch.

"Measure toward the north from that dead tree," Uncle Mel said. He told us how far to go toward the north. He had learned all the measurements.

We measured. At the end of the measurement, we stopped. Where we stopped, there was a big tree.

"That tree must be the marker," Uncle Mel said. "They must have cut that tree to mark the land when it was first measured. Look, men. Here is the mark where this tree was cut."

"But that was done 70 years ago," Father said.

"It is strange what trees can tell us," Uncle Mel said. Tim Mennix, Orbie Dorton, and Dave Sperry were there. They listened. "The mark of a cut will always remain on the outside of the tree and on the inside also. That is how trees remember."

Uncle Mel began cutting into the tree with his ax. He cut out a small piece of wood with each blow. Deep inside the tree he found a dark spot.

"Come, men, and look," Uncle Mel said. "That is where the tree was cut before."

"I think the tree was cut 70 years ago," Orbie Dorton said. "That was when they measured this land."

"We will learn if it was 70 years ago," Uncle Mel said. Inside the tree, in the newly cut wood, there were marks like rings. He began to count these rings, starting at the outside and going toward the center. He counted to the dark spot, deep inside. There were 70 rings between that spot and the outside of the tree.

"Does this tree mark the edge of the land?" Uncle Mel asked.

"It can't do anything else," Dave Sperry said.

We measured again to another tree. It was another marker. Uncle Mel cut into it and counted the rings. There were 70 rings from the outside to the dark spot inside, where the tree had been cut before.

We continued measuring. We found every tree, except one, that was named in my father's deed. That one tree had been cut down. But we found its stump.

"Now we must show a judge what we have found," Uncle Mel said.

Many men came to listen to the judge when he decided about our land. All the other men who had lost land to Jake Timmins were there.

The judge decided. It was our land.

"And the winter food for Jake Timmins' cows belongs to you now," Uncle Mel said. "He put it in your barn. Now I must go home. If you have any more land troubles, write to me."

We wanted him to stay a while. But he would not. He put his ax on his shoulder. We waved good-bye to him as he walked slowly away.

My father walked five miles to work on the railroad. Wood engraving by Mallete Dean.

Chapter 5

A Good Neighbor

The best time of our lives was around our table in the evening. Again our table was filled with food. We were farming our own land. We did not need to pay rent.

At six in the evening, Mother covered our table with food. After school each afternoon, we fed our farm animals. We milked the cows. We cut wood for the kitchen fire. We were always hungry after this work.

We produced almost all our food. We bought only a few things, like salt and sugar.

My father walked five miles to work on the railroad. Then he worked five hours before noon. I got up at four in the morning and helped with the farm work. We both needed a good breakfast by 5 a.m.

My sisters, Glennis and Mary, remained in bed until six. We were never at the table at the same time in the morning.

But in the evening we ate together. Then we talked. Sometimes we all talked at the same time. Then Father stopped us, and only one talked.

These evenings at the table made our family strong. They joined us together. At our table, we made all our plans. We talked about what we hoped to do. Sometimes neighbors came to eat with us.

Sometimes members of Father's or Mother's family came.

The Tillmans came often. We named Fonse Tillman "Uncle Fonse," but he was not our uncle. He was only a good friend of Father's and a neighbor. I remember that Father often said to Mother: "Cook lots of food today! Cook as much as you can. Fonse and Effie are coming and bringing all their children."

I could see that Father was happy. He had a smile on his face from ear to ear. He took his ax and cut wood for the kitchen fire.

Mother cooked a big pot of beans when Uncle Fonse came with his family.

I can remember seeing his mule pulling the heavy wagon up the hill. He pulled and then stopped, took a deep breath, wiggled his ears, and tried again. Father always called: "Fonse, get out and walk."

Then Fonse laughed and Father laughed. And the mule pulled again.

When the mule at last pulled the heavy wagon to

our door, Fonse got out. He slapped Father on the back and Father slapped him. Fonse was big. We were always afraid that he might hurt Father. But they laughed.

Then Father said: "You are getting fat, Fonse. You do not do enough running up and down the hills. Perhaps you eat more than I eat. My wife feeds me only when other people come to eat. That is why I asked you to come today."

Fonse's wife, Effie, went into the house with her seven children.

Father always said to me: "Jesse, you take your Uncle Fonse's mule and feed him. Give him some of that good white corn." Then I took the mule from the wagon. I gave him the white corn. It was better food than we gave our mules. Father always gave his best to Uncle Fonse's mule.

We thought that Father was better to Uncle Fonse's boys than he was to us. We never told him that. But we did not like it. Uncle Fonse's boys were afraid of us. They would not go into the woods to play with us.

James said: "Those boys are not in my family. I do not like them. Dad can't force me to like them. I will throw rocks at them. I will take some skin off that one's head, if I can."

In the kitchen Effie always said: "Let me help you with the dinner, Mrs. Stuart. Let me help with the

While the parents visit, the children play.
Photo by Earl Palmer.

beans. Let me peel the potatoes. Let me do something."

She was very fat. When she moved, her every breath was loud. Mother often told Father after she left: "I can't listen to her when she moves. I told her to sit down and peel the potatoes. She is so fat. I do not understand how she is able to move. I do not understand how she is able to cook for her children. They eat so much. I thought our children could eat a lot. But her children eat more."

I remember what Father and Uncle Fonse always did before dinner. They sat on the floor and talked. Father said: "Fonse, why are we such big fools? Do we belong to the same family?" Then he got up. "I am forgetting something, Fonse." He brought tobacco that he had rolled for smoking.

Uncle Fonse laughed. He said: "You would forget your head if it was not tied on." And then he laughed again. They sat there on the floor, smoking and talking.

They talked about farming. Father often said: "I will have the best corn in Kentucky. It was very cold last winter. That makes the ground better. I will get some good potatoes out of that ground, too. You watch me. I will have more corn than you do this year."

Uncle Fonse said: "You will not do better than any other farmer. But your wife might." And he laughed and Father laughed. Uncle Fonse's fat face and neck shook when he laughed.

Then Mother came to the door and said: "Dinner is ready, Mick. Call the children."

We always came like chickens, running to get their corn in the morning.

Big and small, we sat together. Father and Uncle Fonse talked and laughed. Mother laughed. Effie laughed. All the children laughed, too.

After dinner, Father and Uncle Fonse smoked again. And Mother and Effie smoked. Big clouds of smoke went up from our table. It was not easy to get a breath of good air. I always said: "I will never smoke when I am a man. I do not like tobacco."

Fonse said: "That boy is no Stuart if he does not smoke. His mother, his father, all his uncles—his whole family uses tobacco. Tobacco is a joy to us all."

After they smoked, Father and Uncle Fonse walked toward the fields. Mother and Effie took their chairs and sat under a tree. We children played in the hills.

Uncle Fonse's boys liked my sisters. James and I liked their sisters. We played together happily—running in the sunlight, jumping over the small streams, laughing, and shouting. The time passed quickly.

Then Uncle Fonse and Father returned. Father was little and thin. Uncle Fonse was big and heavy. They came laughing and talking. Father slapped Uncle

Fonse on the shoulder. He said: "This has been a fine day, Fonse. Come again."

And Uncle Fonse always said: "I am never coming again until you bring Sal and all the children to our house."

My brother James and Uncle Fonse's boy, Bill, had the mule and wagon ready. I remember the mule standing beside the flowers. I remember the sun going down beyond the hills, with red clouds above it. I remember Father and Uncle Fonse and Mother helping Effie get into the wagon.

Effie stepped first on a rock, then on a chair, and then into the wagon. The others held her. "I do not want to break a bone at my age," Effie always said.

"And if my wife adds any more pounds," Uncle Fonse said, "she will break the wagon seat. I feed my wife. Look at your wife, Mick. You should feed her better."

After they were gone, Father always said: "Sal, there can be no better neighbor than old Fonse. He does not belong to my Political Party or my Church. He is what he is, and I am what I am. But he is a good neighbor."

"We have good fences between our farms. Good fences make good neighbors."

"But you two act like children when you are together," Mother always said.

"There is something heavy here in my coat," Father said. Then he found a tack hammer that Uncle Fonse had put there. It was something Uncle Fonse had made, something my father needed.

Time passed quickly. I saw the gray hairs come to Father's head. He was growing old. Uncle Fonse was growing old.

Time takes away what can never be returned.

But time could not stop Father and Uncle Fonse from bringing their families together. We had one or two big dinners together every week. Time could not stop them from laughing and talking. They were growing old, but together they seemed young.

I remember Father laughing at the table one morning. He said: "Fonse tried to fool me yesterday. I went to his farm to talk about my boy James and his boy Bill. I heard that they were at that bad dance hall one night. There has been trouble at that place."

I said to Fonse: "What can we do about our boys?" Fonse was getting into his wagon. Fonse said to me: "You take care of the boys, Mick. I won't be here to take care of them after tomorrow night."

"Why? What have you done? Are you leaving Kentucky?"

Fonse said: "No, I have done nothing wrong. I am going to die tomorrow night. It is my heart. I could see it happening when I was in bed last night. I saw the whole thing." And Fonse laughed and laughed.

Father said: "Where are you going now, Fonse?"

"Going to town to have the Jones boys make a coffin for me." And he went down the road. He was laughing. And Father was laughing.

James went to town the next day. When he came home he said to Father: "I believe that Uncle Fonse is going crazy. He told the Jones boys to make a coffin for him. He has had the wood for it for ten years. Ten years ago, he cut down two trees for that wood."

"I was at his house today," James said. "He told me that he expects to die tonight." While I was there he got into the coffin and tried it. "It is a good fit," Fonse said. Bill laughed at his father. The girls cried. Their mother cried.

She said: "He is either telling the truth or he is crazy. And there has never been a Tillman who was crazy."

"He does not seem like a dying man. He will not tell how he knows."

I remember how Father laughed. "He likes to make us laugh. But when he is near dying, he will make his own coffin. He can make anything."

When Father went to bed that night, the wind was blowing through the trees beside the house. I remember seeing him get out of bed in a nightshirt. He looked at the moon and the stars. He walked outside, across the cold ground, without his shoes. That was strange.

I heard him return to the bed. He woke Mother from her sleep. He said: "Sal, I am troubled about Fonse. I can't sleep. I have tried. But I can see a big wooden box in front of me. Get out of bed and make some coffee."

Father put on his clothes. He walked outside, passing the cows and pigs. I heard them make noises as he passed. He was indeed troubled. I saw him like this only once before. That was the night when Brother James was cut in a fight at the dance hall.

I heard Mother call him to get his coffee. I heard him pull his chair to the table. He said to Mother: "I am going to Fonse's place as soon as there is light. I know something has happened."

"I saw Fonse in my mind. I heard him laugh. I swear this is true."

He once said to me: Mick, you ought to be in my church. I will prove it is the right church. If I die before you, go to the forest where we always walked. You will hear me laugh. If you die before me, I will go there and listen.

"I agree, Fonse. If you laugh, I will know that laugh anywhere."

"I went into the pine grove this morning," Father

said. "I have come from there now. I heard old Fonse laugh. I know it was his voice. I know his voice. I know that laugh. I know it was his laugh. It was not the wind. It was his laugh. And I am shaking."

I saw Father go across the hill. He told me to feed the hogs. He told me not to get the mules ready for plowing. He told me to wait.

I saw him go to the top of the hill. He walked beside the fence that he and Uncle Fonse had built. Then he went through the fence and I could not see him.

Mother said: "Perhaps they are both crazy. He said it was not the wind. He said it was Fonse. I do not know what to believe. Perhaps it was the wind."

I felt a strange fear.

When Father returned, Mother ran to meet him.

"Fonse is dead," Father said. "He is as dead as dust. He died last night. The family is crying. I did not stay. I could not. Fonse, quiet, not laughing! But he laughed when he was taking the wood for his coffin to the Jones boys."

"He was not afraid to die. He laughed."

Father was quiet all day. He walked to the forest, then to the house. He watched a bird fly overhead. He looked at the growing corn. He watched the white clouds. He would not let us work. He did not return to the Tillmans' house.

"Thinking about it is strange," said Father. "Life is strange. A man could lose his mind, thinking about it. Fonse has left this earth. He was a good man. He owned land. He sent his children to school. He went to Church. He believed in God. He did not belong to the right Party, but he believed that his Party was right.

"Kentucky needs men like Fonse Tillman. God called him out of this life. But worthless men are allowed to live. I do not understand it. And tomorrow!"

"Yes, tomorrow," said Mother. "They will put him where he wished to be. Near his cornfield. I remember seeing him working up there, behind his mules. I can't forget it."

We were all there. A crowd was there. I remember how Father helped to carry the heavy coffin up the hill.

I remember the flowers in the forest near where they laid Uncle Fonse. The flowers waved in the wind. The quiet crowd left the hill. The wind blew above in the fruit trees.

I looked at the Kentucky hills. The birds were flying over them. Among them, men and women worked for their bread. They knew the change of seasons. They saw life change with the years, sometimes sweetly, and sometimes with great sorrow. They saw flowers open and they saw flowers die.

The hills will remain forever. But no one can stop time.

Uncle Fonse knew when he would die. Now he rests in those Kentucky hills that will remain forever.

If those hills could speak, they could tell more stories than any man can tell. They could tell stories of life, love, dying, darkness, and lost hope. They could tell stories not easy to believe. And their stories would make a book as big as a mountain.

"We made good whiskey in Kentucky."
Photo by Arnold Hanners.

Chapter 6

"Bad To Drink"

Father was a man who liked to drink. Almost all the men in our part of Kentucky liked to drink. Sometimes they promised never to drink again. But the whiskey that we made in Kentucky was very good. They always drank again.

My father often drank with Warfield Flaughtery. When Warfield died, I asked my father what killed him.

"It was drinking," Father said. "He was always bad to drink. After his mother died, he began to drink more. He sold part of his land to buy liquor. He was very bad before he died. He did not remember to feed his animals or milk his cows. Weeds grew tall in his garden."

"Then he was found in his wagon, beside the road. He was not dead, but he was very sick. He had been drinking for 11 days. Friends took him to a doctor, but he died."

I had been away from the hills. I had been in college and in the army. I said: "Things have changed here in the last seven years."

"Yes, they change every year," said Father. "They will never be the same as they were. I do not know what to think. Old Warfield was a drinking man. But he cared for his mother until she died. He believed in God. He never hurt any one except himself."

We went the next morning to dig a grave for Warfield. We stayed to bury him that afternoon.

The crowd gathered. Many came wearing black. I knew most of the old women. They knew the bad and the good of the life among the hills.

There was a good deal of talk about how Flaughtery had lived. The old women spoke about his mother. The men talked about selling his land. They talked of the price it might get.

They put his coffin into the ground. Then the crowd went away.

Warfield Flaughtery was not the only man in our hills who loved to drink. Another was my mother's brother, Uncle Jeff Hilton. He was a very large man. When he was drinking, he made trouble. I remember when I was sent to get him....

"Jesse, I want you to go get Brother Jeff," Mother

said. "He is lying in a barn on Thompson's farm."

"How can I bring him over the mountain?"

"You must pull him on a sled. Get James to help you."

When I went to get the mules to pull the sled, Father said: "Why do you want the mules?"

I told him.

"That will be bad for the mules," Father said.

"It will not be easy for Uncle Jeff," said James.

"Good!" Father said. "He has come to my house only three times. I have been married to his sister 33 years. Twice we pulled him here on a sled. One time we carried him. I would rather have a snake in the house than your Uncle Jeff."

"But Mom is worried about him," I said.

"He is never worried about her," Father said.

James and I now had the mules, Dick and Dinah, ready.

"You will need a strong line," Father said. "You must tie Jeff on the sled or he will roll off like a log."

It was not easy for Dick and Dinah to pull the sled, even without Jeff, over the mountain. And Uncle Jeff weighed more than three hundred pounds.

There was a crowd standing around Uncle Jeff, looking at him. "He has been lying here almost a week," Effie Thompson said. "People come every day to look at him. And he fills the space that belongs to one of my cows. She must stay outside while he is here."

There were two big jugs beside him. One had nothing in it. The other was half full of whiskey.

"Can you help us get him on the sled?" I asked.

"We sure can," Effie Thompson said. "I will be glad to get him out of our barn and bring the cow inside."

We lifted Uncle Jeff on the sled, tied him on, and started home.

Sometimes the sled turned on its side. Sometimes it stood on one end. Sometimes it stood on the other end. Two times it turned upside down. But the line held Uncle Jeff.

There was a new moon in the sky. It gave us enough light.

When we got home, Uncle Jeff could move a little and talk a little. Mother and Father helped him into the house.

"Bad trip," Uncle Jeff said. "Bad to tie a man to a sled and pull him over a mountain."

"Better than you deserve," Father said.

"You do not talk like that when you have been drinking," Mother said to Father.

"When I drink too much, I stay home," Father said.

"But Jeff does not have a home," Mother said.

"Now we have a snake in the house," Father said.

"Your father will discover that Jeff is a worker," Mother said to James and me. Father had gone to bed. "There is only one bad thing about Jeff. His trouble is not women, and it is not fighting. It is drinking."

When Father got up at five the next morning, Uncle Jeff got up, too. When we went to build a fence, Uncle Jeff showed Father how to do it.

"Jeff is a good fence builder," Father told Mother. "And he can do as much work as three men, although he is 60 years old."

That winter he cut wood with us. He could cut as much wood as James, Father, and I, together, could cut. He put iron horse-shoes on the mules' feet. That was something that none of us could do. He was a good mule driver, too.

Uncle Jeff was glad to have a home during the winter. He did not ask to be paid for his work. Father was glad to have his help. He told Mother that Jeff could eat like three men, but he worked like four.

At the end of the winter, Uncle Jeff asked for a dollar for a day's work. Mother and Father agreed that Jeff had changed. He talked about how bad whiskey was. He explained to Mother about how drinking could destroy a man. Father became afraid to drink even a beer.

Uncle Jeff was like a picture of good health. He

weighed more than three hundred pounds. But he was a big man, not a fat man.

Then Father paid Uncle Jeff his first money. Uncle Jeff went to town. He said that he wanted to buy a few little things.

He did not return for two days. "He is drinking," Father said.

Father found him in the early morning, sleeping near the cows. "I came home late. You were all sleeping. I came here because I did not want to make any noise in the house," Uncle Jeff said.

He worked all day in the cornfield. He explained to Father about how bad liquor could be. Father decided that Uncle Jeff had not been drinking in town.

Every week during the summer Uncle Jeff went to town. He was always gone two days. He said he visited one of his children.

James was coming across the mountain when he heard singing. Behind a rock, he found Uncle Jeff and his two big jugs of whiskey. We took the sled and pulled Uncle Jeff home.

That next winter Uncle Jeff did less work. He talked more about how bad it was to drink. Father did not pay him for his work. When the winter ended, Uncle Jeff wanted pay. He asked for three gallons of whiskey every week. We had planted more corn, because we expected his help. He knew that we needed him.

Then we began to hear about what he was doing in town. The town people were talking about him. He was entering strange houses at night when he was drinking. People found him in a bed in the morning. And they were afraid of him.

Father told Mother that he had had enough of Uncle Jeff. He said that either Uncle Jeff was going away, or he himself was going away.

"Jeff has no home," Mother said. "His children will not have him. He is not leaving here."

Father began gathering his clothes together.

"Where are you going, Mick?" Mother asked.

"I am going to the Big Sandy River, among my people."

"When will you return?" Mother asked.

"When Jeff goes," Father said.

Then he told James and me to do the best we could if he never returned. He told us his home was not his home now. We watched him walk slowly down the road, a small sun-browned man, leaving his own home.

As soon as Father left W-Hollow, Uncle Jeff went to town. Mother sat crying. She said that both would return.

That evening Uncle Jeff returned. He had been drinking. He sat down beside the front door. Mother stopped crying when she saw us working, while Uncle Jeff sat there.

"Go away from here, Jeff," Mother shouted. She had an ax handle in her hand. "Take your clothes and go!"

Uncle Jeff went. His clothes, rolled together, were on his shoulder. He carried a jug of whiskey in his hand. He could not walk straight. We watched him go over the hill toward the sunset.

"He is gone," Mother said, crying. "What will happen to him?"

"He will be fine," James said.

"I wish I knew how Dad is," I said.

Mother said nothing.

Summer passed. We heard nothing from Father.

The tobacco needed care. Tall weeds grew in our corn. Our potatoes were still in the ground. James and I worked and worked, but could not get the work finished.

Mother often asked us when we thought Father would return. We said that we did not expect him. Her face was sad.

It was almost winter when he returned. James and I ran to meet him. We expected anger, but he was laughing.

Yes, he returned.

Uncle Jeff lived past 80 years of age. He stopped drinking whiskey.

"Mother often asked us when we thought Father would return."

Jesse's grandfather, Mitchell Stuart.

Chapter 7

The Feud

When I was a little boy, my father and I went to visit my Grandfather Stuart. He lived on a hill near the Big Sandy River. He was sitting outside the house in a big chair. He said to my father: "What are you doing with the boy, Mitch? Are you letting him grow up like a weed?"

He pulled me close to him, and rubbed his closed, hard fist across my head. It hurt, and I cried and tried to get away. I was afraid of him. He was very big and had a long beard.

He pointed to the Big Sandy River, and said: "Never no more, Mitch, will I ride logs down the river. That river is as dear to me as my blood. But my life is coming to an end, Mitch. See my white hair. My legs are weak. Time always catches a man."

When we went away my father said: "Son, you see that fence up there on the hill. My father built it there when I was a little boy. My sister Belle carried me there on her back." The fence was still standing and it seemed as strong as a new fence.

I asked my father how many men my grandfather had killed. He had killed men in the Civil War in the years 1861 to 1865. But he had killed others, too.

My father said: "Do not ask so many questions son, children should be seen and not heard."

I learned about a man who was hunting to kill Grandfather. When Grandfather heard about him, he started hunting the man who was hunting him. He found his own brother, Uncle Bob, and thought that he was the man. He almost killed him.

The man hunting Grandfather was killed that same night. That night another man left the Big Sandy River valley. Everyone thought that he was the killer. Nothing more happened. There was no trial in Court.

My father often said: "There never was another worker like my father. He cut down more trees than any other man in the Big Sandy River valley. He could cut the trees from 30 acres of land in a year. In three years, he could have the land ready to farm, with a house and fence on it."

"As soon as his corn and tobacco were gathered, he began cutting trees. In the winter when the ground was cold and hard, he pulled the logs to the river."

"All of us children worked from daylight until dark. Every person near Dad worked. He was a big

"Son, you see that fence up there on the hill. My father built it..."

Photo by Arnold Hanners.

Log run on the Big Sandy River.
Photo by Arnold Hanners.

powerful man with little hands and little feet."

That was the first time my father took me to see Grandfather. The last time he took me, Grandfather was dead.

"Dad will never ride logs down the river again," My father said. "They tied the logs together, and we could ride on them. I went with him many times when I was a little boy. I have seen a big log break away from the others. And I have seen my father jump on it. Sometimes he fell into the water. But he always brought the log back."

"It is strange to remember these things. I feel strange."

The sun went down and the deep valley was dark. Here and there we could see a light in a house. We were riding on a railroad car beside the river.

"Will someone meet us?" I asked my father.

"Some one will be there," he said. "Stuarts will be returning here from everywhere."

"When will they bury him?" I asked.

"Quiet!" he said. He looked over his shoulder.

I saw two men with long beards listening.

"You never know here," my father said, "if you are talking near a friend or an enemy."

The two men stood up and followed us when our railroad trip ended.

"Are you going to see Mick Stuart buried?" one of

the men asked Father. "Mick" was the name used by my grandfather, too.

"That is where we are going," Father said. "Are you a member of the family?"

"We are his brother's children," the man said. "I am Zack Stuart. This is my brother, Dave. We are Zack Stuart's boys."

"I am Mick Stuart," Father told them. "I am the last of Dad's 11 children by his first wife."

"We have heard about you," Zack Stuart said. "We left the Big Sandy a long time ago. Why did you leave?"

"Trouble with the Hornbuckles," Father said.

"Trouble with the Hornbuckles and Dangerfields caused us to leave," Dave said.

"How did your father die?" Zack Stuart asked Father.

"I do not know yet, but I know he did not die of sickness," Father said. "He had more enemies than he had sickness."

"You are right," said a voice from the darkness. "I am Keith Stuart, son of Jimmy Stuart, first son of Mick Stuart. I have come to meet any and all Stuarts and tell them where to go."

"Then Dad was killed?" Father asked Keith Stuart, who, seemed as big as a mountain. "He was beaten to death with a club," Keith told us. "You will see."

"Who killed him?" Dave Stuart asked.

"We know, but we are not saying now," Keith said. "Two men did it. We have men hunting them tonight. You may hear about two dying before tomorrow morning."

"It makes my blood boil," Father said. "But I have been expecting this for many years. He has been fighting a long war."

"We are all angry," Keith said. "We must go. Come with me."

"Do you have a light?" Father asked. "I can't see well in the dark."

"You can't have a light, Uncle Mick," Keith said. "Do you want to be shot?"

"I have been away a long time," Father said. "I forgot. But I remember now."

And I, too, remembered. I remembered Father's stories as we sat around the fire on winter nights. He had told about walking without a light. Men had hunted him because he was a son of old Mick Stuart. He had been shot at many times. Shots had come very near him.

"No talking here," Keith told us. "Be quiet until I tell you when to talk."

We were quiet. We walked holding hands, with Keith leading us. He had been on this road often, and he could feel it with his feet.

I was glad that my father had left the Big Sandy River valley. I was glad that he had gone to the Little Sandy River. I was glad that I was born there.

Grandfather had been a soldier. He had been in the Civil War from beginning to end.

But after he returned home, he was in a war that never ended. His enemies were men who had not been soldiers in the War. They had remained in the Kentucky hills. During the War, they did many bad things; they killed and destroyed and took the belongings of men who were away fighting the War. Grandfather had been fighting these men since 1865, except during three years when he lived near the Little Sandy River.

They had said that they would kill him. And now they had done it.

"We can talk now," Keith said. "We have passed the Hornbuckle and Dangerfield farms."

"When will they bury him?" Father asked.

"Two in the morning," Keith said.

I could understand why they were doing this in darkness. We were among enemies. In every part of the Stuart family, except my father's, one, two, or three men had been killed by our enemies. Why did we have so many enemies?

"I will tell you what Dad did wrong," my father said. "His second wife belonged to the Dangerfield and the Hornbuckle families. I cannot understand why he married an enemy!"

I did not know we were near Grandfather's house. There was no light from any window. Keith knocked at the door three times. Father's brother, Uncle Jim, opened it.

Now, for the first time, I saw my father's people. Many of them had been hurt in the long War. After I looked at them, I was glad I lived far away.

We followed Keith into the room where Grandfather lay. He pointed to the blue marks across Grandfather's face. He opened his coat and shirt and showed us the marks on his body. I had never seen a man beaten as he had been beaten—this man who had died in a battle he had been fighting 46 years.

Uncle Jason came into the room. "It is time for us to start," he said. Six of my uncles lifted the coffin and carried Grandfather out into the night. They were tall men with big shoulders.

The crowd of Stuarts followed. Keith led us up the mountain. The moon came out behind the mountain top.

None of Grandfather's eight children by his second wife were there. "I am glad," Uncle Cief told Father. "They have enemy blood in them."

I was with my people and it seemed like a dream. I had not known that there was a world like this.

We stopped on the lonely mountain top. I could see the waiting hole in the ground. An owl passed over our heads. On a distant mountaintop, a whippoorwill called. It was a lonely sound. There was not a light nor a sound among us as Grandfather's body was placed beside his grave.

Now an old soldier, an old friend of my grandfather, spoke. "Tonight we are putting an old soldier in his grave," he said. "He was fighting a long war in the land of his enemies, and he has fought a good fight."

Two men walked through the crowd and toward the old soldier. Uncle Cief's gun was ready, until he knew who they were.

They spoke quietly to the old soldier, and he spoke again. "I am glad to tell you that the enemy has paid for killing Mick Stuart. Eif Dangerfield and Battle Henson paid for what they did!"

That was all that was said. Grandfather's coffin was placed in the ground on a mountain top among other Stuart graves. It was a high mountain, looking down on the hills where our people and our enemies lived.

Mitchell Stuart's brother, Uncle Jim.

Working on the railroad.
Wood engraving by Mallete Dean.

Chapter 8

Uncle Jeff

I had two Uncle Jeffs. One was my mother's brother, and the other was my father's brother. Uncle Jeff Stuart was like all the Stuarts: he was a strong man and a worker. At the end, suddenly, all his strength was gone.

Uncle Jeff was a good man. I remember him best as he was when I saw him last. And I remember how my father felt....

Father and James and I were in a big city, Huntington, West Virginia. We were going to visit Uncle Jeff. He was ill. He was in a railroad hospital, where doctors care for sick railroad workers. Uncle Jeff was probably dying.

Father did not like the city. He could not read the names of the streets. He had to ask people where to go. He was taking us because we could read. We were glad to go with him.

"What is Uncle Jeff's sickness, Dad?" I asked. "Why is he dying?"

"He has used all his strength," said Father. "He is like I am. Look at me. If you had worked a long time on the railroad, then you, too, would have one foot in the grave and the other foot ready to follow. He has worked on the railroad 33 years."

"He could have had a better job, if he could read. Like me. Now you boys understand why you should go to school. There was no school in the Kentucky hills when I was a boy."

"Brother Jeff is like an old horse that can't pull the plow. But he must pull it. He is like I am. I have not the strength to pull the plow, but I must pull it anyhow."

James read the street names. He had been to school and he could read quite well.

People looked at us, and Father did not like it. He was not as big as we were. He walked between us. He was wearing a big long gray coat. It came almost to his feet. I found it in an old house where no one lived.

Father said: "This is a big city. Look at these big houses. It costs money to build them. Boys, look at these houses!"

We arrived at the hospital. James and I walked in behind Father. A nurse was sitting at a table, writing. Father said: "Is Jeff Stuart here? I want to see him."

"He is very sick. No one can visit him," said the

woman.

"What?" said Father. "A man comes 40 miles and can't see his dying brother!"

"You cannot see him," said the woman.

I saw Father becoming angry. James took his arm and said: "We will find the doctor. He will let us see Uncle Jeff."

We found the doctor. "You want to see Jeff Stuart?" said the doctor. "It is good that you have come to see him. None of his family have come. I am afraid he will not return to Kentucky alive."

He took us to Uncle Jeff's room. He opened the door and walked away.

Father went in first. "Hello, Jeff," he said. "Do you know me?"

"Know you?" said Uncle Jeff. "What do you think I am? I would know you anywhere, Mick. And you have come to see me die."

"I have come to see you," said Father.

"I am dying," said Uncle Jeff. Then he saw James. "Come here and say good-bye. And you," he said pointing to me, "come here and say good-bye to your Uncle Jeff."

I wished that Uncle Jeff would not hold my hand. He was holding my hand and talking to Father. His hand was soft and warm and old. His eyes were blue and very old.

"That nurse," said Uncle Jeff, "is trying to kill me. I want to go home to die. I want to die where Dad and Mom died."

"Lie still in the bed, Jeff," Father was saying. "Then you will soon be well. You will go home next week."

"You know I am never going home, Mick. And I know it. I am sorry to leave my little children."

I said to my brother James: "I remember Uncle Jeff when he was young. I remember his first wife, as pretty as any woman in Kentucky. They had three children, three girls. Then she died. Uncle Jeff cared for those girls until they married."

"Then he was alone. He married again. An old man and a young woman. You see what happens."

Uncle Jeff was talking loud. "You always got anything you wanted. You were Mother's baby."

"That is right," said Father. "I was her last-born."

"That nurse is coming," said Uncle Jeff. "I do not want her in this room, Mick."

"These people must go now," said the nurse. "You must take your medicine. It will help you to feel better."

"I do not want to drink that. I would rather die. I may not go to heaven. I am not a very good man. But I have not been a very bad one. I never was certain about what was good and what was bad."

"Will you drink this?" asked the nurse.

"No."

"You will die!"

"That is what I expect to do and what you will do, too."

But the doctor came in. "My good man, take your medicine," he said.

"Do not send that woman in here again," Uncle Jeff said. "She does not understand about anything."

The doctor laughed and said: "No, she does not understand about anything."

"Now, Mick," Uncle Jeff said to Father, "you are going home. We will not meet here again." Father tried to dry his eyes with one hand, and with the other he held Uncle Jeff's old hand.

"Good-bye, Uncle Jeff," I said.

"Good-bye, Uncle Jeff," said James.

"Never work on no railroad," said Uncle Jeff to us.

We walked out holding Father. "Look at Brother Jeff," he said. "He is a dying man. He worked on the railroad 33 years. I have worked 19. Look at me. My strength is gone. I never was as strong as Jeff. Jeff was the best man among us."

We rode the bus toward home.

Father said: "Work not done. Now it is dark. We have 30 more miles to ride and four miles to walk after we leave the bus."

We walked across the quiet, cold earth and we

were home again. The stars were shining in the sky. We fed the cows and the mules. We brought in wood for the fires.

"Jeff and I did this work when we were boys," said Father. "But we will never do it again together. I will be the next to die. If you boys work on a railroad, I will return from the grave to tell you to stop. You get small pay and do the most work. I have worked more than a man should."

"This is a bad world. There is enough for all, but it is not easy to get a share. I can't get it, nor can other men like me. I can't read. I never went to school."

The next afternoon, rain fell. Black clouds hung low over the forest. We received the news that Uncle Jeff was dead. "I expected it," said Father.

Father prepared to go to Uncle Jeff's funeral. He wore his old blue suit—his best suit. He wore one of James's shirts and a black hat. He walked out into the rain. He was going by railroad to the Big Sandy Valley.

He could ride on the railroad without paying. But he must ride in a car for poor people. Father was poor. That was where he expected to ride.

We did not want to go with Father. Uncle Jeff's house was small. There was no place for us to sleep. Uncle Joe lived near, but we could not sleep at his house. Uncle Joe and Uncle Jeff had trouble. The women they married fought with each other. Uncle Joe and Uncle Jeff stopped speaking to each other a few months before Jeff died.

A month before that, James and I went to Uncle Jeff's house. Father, Uncle Joe, Uncle Jeff, James and I all went to find my father's mother's grave.

We went through thick forest. "Here," said Uncle Joe, "I often carried you, Mick. And Jeff also. Corn was growing here then. Our father built that fence."

My father stopped and picked up a fence rail. "He worked and worked, and died poor," he said.

We gathered wild flowers as we walked. Father, Uncle Jeff, and Uncle Joe also gathered flowers.

"This is the right road," said Uncle Joe. "But I have not gone to Mother's grave since we put her there. I never wanted to return to it. But I remember the road. We must turn here."

The trees seemed very old to me. "And Grandpa had cut down all the trees here?" I asked. "Corn grew here?"

"Yes," said Uncle Joe.

Soon we came to a hillside with a few trees. "There is where she lies," said Uncle Joe. But they were not certain which grave was hers.

They asked an old farmer, who owned the next farm. "There are 11 graves there," he said. "Your mother is in the middle. She is number six."

We put our flowers there.

Uncle Jeff said: "We three brothers are now her only living children. I shall be the next to come here. And I want to lie under this fruit tree. Remember that, Mick."

Then I understood. Uncle Jeff would lie where the flowers fell from that fruit tree. No sound of the railroad would come to him there.

"I hope there is soft ground to plow in Heaven."
Photo by Earl Palmer.

Chapter 9

Home From College

I was homesick. I wanted to see the house that I had helped to build. I wanted to see my father's land.

It was winter. He showed me the corn, in the barn where it was stored. "It was a good season, Jesse," he said. "But we needed you. I do not know how we did everything without you. I plowed at night when I came home from work on the railroad. I worked by moonlight."

"I think you have done very well. The corn is fine. And see those potatoes!"

"Your mother worked and Mary and James worked in the fields. They are good workers. I do not like to see your mother work in the fields. But if I had a million dollars, she would do it. She will not stay inside the house. Did you see her flowers? They are more work, but I help her with them. She likes them."

"I try to get her anything she wants. She has worked and worked, Jesse, and I have worked. Now we are old. We can't work as we once did."

I could see how the years had marked my father's face. I could see that the best part of his life and strength was gone.

"I was told that you have 50 more acres of hill land," I said.

"That is true."

"Why do you need it? You have done enough work trying to pay for this 50 acres. You will kill yourself paying for more."

"I know what I am doing. I need that land. I love land. I can't get enough of it. I am growing tobacco. I will stop working on the railroad. I expect to die on this farm. I love it here."

The next day we were together again.

"Dad, how is our dog?"

"That dog is the best dog in these hills. We could not live without him. He is as good a hunting dog as he was when you hunted with him. He kills snakes, and we have a lot of snakes here."

"Jesse, this is a fine morning. Let's take our dog and go hunting."

My father shot more rabbits than I did. "Books have changed you," Father said. I think he was right. I did not enjoy hunting and killing as I had before.

I returned to college. When I finished my studies, I became a schoolteacher. Then I became the school principal. I wanted to learn even more, so I returned to college. My brother James went to college when he was 15 years old.

But in the summers we both came home and worked. I remember those summer days with James and my father. I remember well...

"Get up, James," I heard my father say. "Get up before I throw some cold water on you!"

Oh, that voice of my father's! How many times it got me up! I was glad to hear it again. I said: "James, get up!"

"You are here!" James said. "Fine! We have enough work for you. We have more work than five men can do."

"What time is it?" I asked.

"Three in the morning. You know what time Dad gets up."

The moon was low over the mountains. A few whippoorwills called from the hill tops. Bright stars filled the sky.

We met my father. He was coming with cold water for James.

I said: "How would you like to have another man to work here?"

"When did you come? I never heard you. Never needed you so much. There are weeds in the corn and the tobacco. There was only James to fight them. Your mother helps. I work four days each week on the railroad."

"Good morning," Mother said, when I walked into the kitchen. "I am glad you have come. The work here never ends. You seem well. Have you had enough to eat?"

"Oh, yes. I always get enough to eat," I said.

We ate. The stars were shining. My father got a lantern to carry as he walked across the hills to the railroad. "You boys get the weeds out of the corn on the hill today. Sorry you must work on your first day home, Jesse. But we need you."

"Let's get our hoes and begin," James said.

"We must feed the livestock first," I said.

"Dad has already done that. He gets up and makes a fire in the kitchen and then feeds the cows and mules. He is an early bird."

After supper, Father went to the fields and worked until dark. He looked at the corn, where we had been working, and said: "Look at that corn! How pretty it is now!"

He looked at the tobacco. "If it is good, things will be fine. If it is bad this year, I will lose part of my farm. You have done the most important work in the corn. The next work there will be easy. Now we must start with the tobacco."

Two days each week he worked with us.

The sun was hot. It was like a fire over our heads.

"Weeds die quickly on a day like this," Father said to me. We walked up the hill and he took a big red bandanna to dry his neck.

James came, riding the mule. Today he will plow and Father and I will use the hoes.

Our hoes struck against the weeds and the rocks. The dust flew up in little clouds. The wind blew the dust into our eyes. The sun burned down on our backs.

"James, is it time to have a little drink?" asked Father.

"When you are ready," said James, "I am ready." He walked across the dry soil. Dust flew when he lifted his feet. He stopped where a small stream came from the ground.

I saw James lift a big white jug with a brown top. He brought it to Father.

"This is good on a hot day," said Father. He drank.

"Give me a drink," said James. He drank. "Have a drink, Jesse."

"I do not like it, James."

"He is one of God's oddlings," said Father. "There is something strange about Jesse. He thinks about books and writing."

Father drank again and then he gave the jug to James. "Take another drink, son. And then put it in the water where it will be cool."

The tobacco was pretty in long rows where we had cut the weeds. The cut weeds were drying in the sunlight. The wind was not blowing much. But it was moving more quickly than James. But James would move more quickly now.

Father said: "There is a boy that likes what I like. We like to take a little drink without your mother knowing. She says it is bad on a hot day. But she is wrong. If she was right, it would have killed me long ago."

Father was working more quickly now. James was moving more quickly. Father was hot. Sweat ran from his face and body.

"Men today are not like the men who lived long ago," said Father. "I am not a man equal to my father. He could drink more than me, cut down more trees, fight better. He was a real man. I am not as big as my sons. But I can do more work than they can do. You boys can read and write, but I can do everything else better."

"Dad, now you are feeling that drink," said James.

"Granddad cut down the trees," I said. "He built houses. He helped to fight a war for the nation and several wars at home. But look at his work today! The forest covers his fields. The houses are falling down. What is the good of all this work—"

"You are one of God's oddlings, son. You won't

drink. You won't smoke tobacco. You are not like your people. You will become weak and wise."

"You need a strong body and a weak mind to do this work," said James. "The mule knows more than we do. He would not work if we did not force him to do it."

"I grow this tobacco for money," said Father. "Tobacco needs care during the whole year. The work is never finished. And sometimes we get no money for it."

"Did we get any money for tobacco last year?" I asked.

"It cost money to send it to market. It cost money to sell it. When it was sold, the man had no money to give me. And he asked me to pay him 35 cents more. I have not paid him yet."

I looked at the rows of tobacco. They were pretty in the sun and wind. Our hoes shone in the sun. The sun was low. The sun was a fire, trying to burn us and burn the tobacco.

"After we eat," said Father, "we shall return and work some more."

"You should not do this work. You are not strong enough," I said.

"James and I find strength in our drink down there in the cool water. I do as much work as I can, and then I let the drink help me to continue working."

Father's clothes were as full of water as if he had been in the Little Sandy River. His face was dusty. The skin of his hands was thick and hard as the skin of a tree. His neck was red. James's face was gray.

But I felt more sorry for the mule than for James. He had not been able to tell James that he needed water. He could only pull the plow.

"I hope there is soft ground to plow in Heaven," said Father.

The sun was behind the mountains. The sky was red. "It is cool now," said James.

"It has been very hot for plowing. But we have done a lot of work today."

Father said to me: "You are an oddling. Books. Books. Books are not real life. Books are dry as dry soil."

"Look behind us," he said. "Look at the dead weeds. I like to look at the living weeds, also. I want to hoe them down. Tomorrow we will do it. Get the jug, James. You can get it more easily than I can. My legs are not as good as they were when I was young."

James came up the hill with the jug. He came up more slowly than he went down. "We should plant potatoes on this hill. They would be easy to gather. We would take out the bottom row, and the others would all fall out, following them."

Father drank. James drank and drank.

"Son, if you and I go to Heaven and we must plow new ground, what shall we do without some of this whiskey?" He started down the hill. "Time to go, boys."

"I will not ride Old Dick now," James said. "He has worked more than any of us. And he is not interested in tobacco."

"Is that what you think?" said Father. "You do not know much about Dick. Mart Henson's wagon got caught in a hole there on the hill. His mules could not pull it out. He wanted to start a fire under them, so that they would move, but his wife said no."

I went there. I said, "Mart, I have one mule that will pull that wagon out of there."

He said to me, "I will give you 25 dollars if he does. And if he can't do it, you give him to me."

I agreed. I got Dick. He pulled, but the wagon did not move. Mart laughed. "He is my mule," he said.

I remembered that Old Dick and I were good friends. He often followed me across a field for a little piece of tobacco. I said to Mart, "Give me some tobacco." He gave me a little bag of it.

I took it and I stood in front of the mule with it. I saw more pulling then than I ever saw before in all my life. That wagon began to move and it came up out of that hole. And I gave Dick the whole bag of tobacco.

That 25 dollars helped to pay for my land.

That mule loves tobacco. I give him some every morning. "You have surely seen him following me across a field?"

"Yes," I said.

"He was asking for tobacco. Any person or animal will want it after they have a taste of it. When your mother was a little girl, she had a taste of the smoke. After she married me, she did not want me to know. But I knew."

I found her smoking behind the house and I said to her, "Sal, smoke in the house. Why should you not like tobacco?" James was smoking when he was five years old. I knew it.

"I hear Mom calling us to eat," I said. "We must hurry."

"You are an oddling," said Father. "God has many oddlings. Some day you will smoke tobacco. You are a Stuart. All Stuarts smoke tobacco. Your books will not stop you from it."

Father walked slowly toward the house. James led Dick. Behind me, I saw the moon come over the field. I saw the tobacco plants under the light of the moon. They were pretty. The hill was clean of weeds.

The moon was always pretty in Kentucky.

"Some day you will smoke tobacco... All Stuarts smoke tobacco."

Father and his mule.

Chapter 10

Men and Mules

Time Passed. I plowed. I planted seeds. I read books. I did some writing. My father and I took long walks through the woods.

He loved the soil. He loved the trees. He wanted to own more land. Before the end of the summer, he had another 50 acres. He wanted to make a new farm, and then another.

Then Old Dick died.

Before daylight I heard someone calling at my door. When I opened the door, Father was standing there.

"Old Dick is sick," he said. "Will you take me in your car to get a doctor?" "

What is wrong with him, Dad?" I asked.

"I do not know. For 17 years I have gone every morning at four to feed Dick and Dinah. They have always been standing, waiting for me. This morning Dick was lying down. He tried to stand but he could not. Something hurts him. It hurts Dinah to see him.

She can't eat."

"Do I have time to eat before we go?" I asked.

"I have not had anything to eat either," Father said. If we get a doctor quickly, maybe we can save Old Dick."

He wanted me to hurry. And I hurried. I started the car.

"This is a bad time for Dick to be sick," I said. "The roads are mud."

There were chains on the wheels, to help move the car in the mud.

We used the car lights, but I could not see all the holes. It was a bad ride.

We arrived at Wash Nelson's house. "Wash," Father said, "we have a sick mule. Can you come and try to help him?"

In three minutes, Wash was in the car. There was another bad ride. The car moved like a small ship in a storm at sea.

When we arrived at my home, Uncle Jesse was standing at the gate waiting for us. He said, "Old Dick is dead."

After I took Wash back home, I stopped at my home to eat. Then I went to where Father and Uncle Jesse were looking at Old Dick.

There lay Old Dick. It was the first time that I had ever seen him lie perfectly still.

The old men were not talking. But Dinah was. I walked inside the building and looked at her. She had not been eating. For the first time in 17 years, Dick was not at her side.

Yesterday I had seen Dick and Dinah running across the hill. They were playful. They knew each rock and tree, each deep hole of water in the little streams.

When I walked outside the building, Dinah tried to follow me. But she was tied. She began kicking, trying to knock down the wall behind her.

"Dinah, stop that," I shouted. But she did not stop.

Mort Higgins came down the road. "Lost a mule, Mick?" he asked. "I am sorry."

"Yes, I lost a real mule," Father spoke softly.

"I can tell you how to escape the trouble, work, and time of putting him underground," Mort said. "I am going to town. I will have the dead wagon come out here and get that mule."

"Mort, I feel like hitting you with my fist," Father said. "You are a good neighbor, but you do not understand how I feel about that mule."

"Oh, I did not know that you felt like that," Mort said. "I am sorry that I spoke about the dead wagon."

"This mule," Father said, "will be buried here on this farm. He is a part of this farm. It belongs to him as much as it belongs to me. He has worked 17 years for me. He will lie here now that he is dead."

Mort knew that he had said the wrong thing. He turned and left us without saying another word.

Uncle Jesse stood there. He did not say anything. It was the first time I had ever seen him cry. He had worked on the farm, using Old Dick and Dinah, while I was in college. I had seen him driving them four days ago.

Old Dick could pull anything. He failed only once. That time his head was turned away from home. When his head was turned toward home, he never failed.

"Where is a good place to put him, Uncle Jesse?" Father asked.

"I have been thinking about that," Uncle Jesse said.

I said, "There is a good place up there beside that tree."

"The young mules could not pull him up that hill," Uncle Jesse said.

"Old Dick is a big mule. He must weigh 1100 pounds. That is more than the young mules can pull."

"Old Dick could have pulled that much," Father said.

Drops of cool rain started falling.

"There is a good place at the bottom of that little hill," Uncle Jesse said. "It is near the pine grove. Old Dick and Dinah rested there in the summer when they were not working. I think Old Dick liked that place more than any other."

"Yes, I think that is the right place," Father said.

Two neighbors helped me dig the grave. It was raining more. Before we had finished, Father and Uncle Jesse came, driving the young mules down the hill. They were bringing Old Dick. There was a chain around his back legs. They were pulling him like a log.

"Mules understand everything," Father said. "These young mules know that Old Dick is dead."

"Listen to old Dinah," I said.

"She broke her ties and came out of the building two times," Uncle Jesse said. "She ran to Old Dick. We put her inside again. I do not think that she can break the ties now."

Her voice was loud and sad. If mules could cry, she was crying.

The young mules pulled Old Dick to the edge of the hole. And now Dinah was quiet.

"She has learned that she can't come out," Father said.

And then we saw her. She was following us like a dog, with her nose on the ground. She came near, and stood looking at Old Dick.

The young mules, too, were watching. The three mules watched as we lifted Dick's feet and rolled him into the hole. Dinah came to the edge of the hole and looked down.

More tears fell from Uncle Jesse's eyes. Father put a red bandanna to his eyes. Then he began to drive the young mules up the hill.

We covered Old Dick with dirt. When Dinah could not see him, she turned and followed the young mules. She seemed to understand.

Chapter 11

A Road To W-Hollow

When we got our little farm, Father and Uncle Martin Hilton made plans for a road. They planned a route. Then we cut the trees. Then we leveled the ground.

It was a road with many turns. It was not good enough for a car. But we could drive a wagon to our house.

At the end of that winter, we had three days of rain. The rain destroyed our road.

We had put more hard work into building that road than we had while building our house. Now we had lost almost three years of work.

"You will never get a road for us, Mick," Mother said.

"Do not lose hope, Sal," he said. "I have another plan."

Then we tried to build a road across Uncle Martin's farm.

But this road went across a mountain. Very strong

mules were needed to pull a wagon up that mountain. And they could pull the wagon only with nothing in it.

We had worked a year, building this road. We had used all the time when we were not doing farm work. Now all that work was lost.

Another road could have been built along the mountain top. But at the end, the road must go down from the mountain. And it would not be possible for mules to pull a wagon down. The heavy wagon would move too fast. We could not hold it, so that it would move slowly. It would rush down on the mules.

We could have built a good road at the bottom of the valley. But the land belonged to our neighbor, Ben Leadingham. He would not allow us to build a road across his good bottom land.

In 1926 I finished my studies at Greenup County High School. I had worked on two of the roads. We had worked days, evenings, moonlight nights, and we had failed.

I was leaving W-Hollow. I would not work on any more roads. I would let my father continue. He had not lost hope.

I was away from home four years. When I returned, I walked.

The road was bad, as it had been when I left. I saw some strange marks on it. It seemed that a car had used it. It also looked like a sled had used it.

"Jesse, we could not make a good road to this house," Father said. "So I have made something to travel on a bad road. I can bring home supplies now. Come. Let me show you."

It was strange. I had never seen anything like it. It was half wagon and half sled. The wheels were wheels from a car.

"Where did you get it?" I asked.

"Brady Callihan sold it to me," he said. "Brady used it to bring corn from that hill on his farm. He brought wood from the forest. Useful," he said, smiling. "One mule can pull it on a good road. It is perfect for my road."

"But the road goes across the Seaton land," I said. "They can close the road if they want to."

My father was waiting for me to agree that his wagon-sled was wonderful. "What do you think of it?" he said.

"But we need a road," I said. "There is only one good place for it. Through Ben Leadingham's farm."

"Oh, I forgot to tell you," he said. "Ben is dead."

"Who owns the farm now?" I asked.

"Uncle Bill Burgess. But he will never allow us to build a road across his land."

Now our farm was more beautiful than ever. It produced more. My father had made our home a good place to live. My father, mother, brother, and sisters loved this piece of earth. It was the only land we had ever owned. My grandfather and I had built the house with our own hands.

But the high hills were our enemy. And the only neighbor who could help us would not allow us to go across his land.

In 1936, it was 15 years since we had built the house. We still did not have a road. I was now Superintendent of the Greenup County Schools. I had become a writer, too.

I was earning enough money so that I could save some for the future. And Uncle Bill Burgess was old. He wanted to sell his farm.

"Yes, I will sell this farm for 1700 dollars," he told Father. "I want 900 in the first payment. Then the buyer can pay 200 each year until it is all paid."

Father came to tell me. "We can get it, Jesse!" These were his first words. "Two other people have gone to talk about buying it. But they did not have 900 dollars."

I returned with Father. We tried to arrive at Uncle Bill's place before dark. But stars were in the sky when we arrived at his house. He was in bed. He told us to come back the next morning.

I stood at my father's side. We were near a fence. Below us was the Burgess land. It was the only possible place for a good road to our farm.

The soil was dark and fertile. There were 20 acres

of level bottom land and 80 acres of hills. We had 152 acres of land on our farm. Only two acres were level land.

My father said: "Jesse, if we owned that land, we would have bottom land to farm, and a road. Your mother has always wanted that land."

My father had rented some of that land. My mother had worked there for 25 cents for a day's work. He and his horse had worked there for one dollar and 50 cents per day. I had worked there for 25 cents per day. But it was land we could not go across.

I also wanted that land. I did not tell him, but I had been saving money to buy that land and then build a road to our door.

We had been fenced in for 16 years.

The next morning, bright and early, we were at Uncle Bill's house. I agreed to pay the $1700. We agreed to meet the next day in Greenup and finish our business.

The next day I took my 900 dollars. I made the first payment on the farm. Now I owned land where we could build the only possible road to my family's home. Already, while I was making that payment, Father was working on the road.

He was cutting through fences. Four men were helping him. They were cutting trees to make bridges. They had to build eight bridges. But we knew that now we had our road!

"You have got the land," Father said. "And I will build the road."

He did. Before the next summer, he had finished it.

To other people this might not have seemed a good road. But we thought that it was the best road in America.

Years passed before our road was graded. I remember that in the middle of World War II, Father continued to work on our road. There was still not a good public road into W-Hollow.

"There is something I want you boys to remember," Father said. "We want Toodle Powell to be the next Greenup County judge."

"Dad," James said, "I must return to the war."

"And I must go also," I said.

"He will be the best judge we have had in Greenup," Father said. "He belongs to the Right Party. He is a big man!"

"He truly is a big man," James said, laughing. "What does he weigh?"

"Do not laugh," Father said. "I have been talking

"Dad," James said, "I must return to the war." "And I must go also," James said. From left, Mitchell and Martha, and their children Jesse, Sophie, Mary, James and Glennis.

to Toodle Powell. When he is judge, we won't sit here in mud holes. He will give us a road in every valley. And it will be a good, hard, stone road. You boys know that the Wrong Party never made us a good road. We had mud roads while they ruled!"

"If Toodle Powell becomes judge, we will continue to have mud roads," James said. "Don't tell me he can put a good road in every valley. He could not do it in ten years!"

"Old Toodle can do anything!" Father's face was red with anger. "He is a great man. He is the best man in the Right Party."

"I will do what I can to help, Dad," I said.

James and I returned to the war. Soon the war ended. But neither James nor I could return home for a while. During this time, Toodle Powell was indeed elected the judge in Greenup County.

I returned in the middle of winter. There had been some warm weather. The mud in all the valley roads was very bad. I waited in Greenup for cold weather to freeze the mud, so I could drive my car.

My father learned that I was in Greenup. He walked across the mountain to see me.

"Jesse," Father said, "now is the time to go to Judge Toodle Powell. This is his first day as judge. We want that road! This will be the last time that you must wait for cold weather! Now the Right Party is the ruling party."

Father was very happy. He was 67 years old, but as we walked along the street, he jumped into the air, cracking his heels together. He did this again and again. He talked so fast about Toodle Powell and the members of the Right Party, that I could not ask about Mother's health. I could not ask about the farm, or about our house.

Judge Toodle Powell was in a large room filled with people.

"Why are all these people here?" I asked Father. "Do they all want roads?"

A big man behind me said, "You are right. We all want roads. And we will get them now!"

Everywhere in the crowd we could hear the word "road."

And there sat Judge Toodle Powell. There was a smile on his face. His big blue eyes seemed to smile, too. It was easy to see that he was a very important and powerful man.

Hours passed before it was our time to say what we wanted.

I stood up and said that I was waiting for the road to freeze. I said that I wanted to take my wife and daughter home in my car.

People laughed. I heard them say that we could walk home, as they did. They said that the war had made me weak.

But Judge Toodle said: "Jesse, you know that we can't work on that road now. But that is an important road. We will be there as soon as the weather will let us."

"Good enough, Judge Powell," Father said. "We know that you will do what you promise."

As we walked away, Father said: "I hope that we have the road before James comes home. He doubted Toodle Powell!"

I waited two more days before I could drive home. And I was able to drive the car to Greenup only two times that winter. I had to walk across the mountain, carrying some of our supplies. We used a wagon pulled by four mules for our heavy supplies.

Father and I went two more times to talk to Judge Powell about our road.

"You will have that road, Mick," Judge Powell promised us. "We will put gravel on it and a black top."

"A black-topped road in W-Hollow!" Father said as we returned across the mountain. "That is a big change in 50 years."

"It will be," I said, "if we get the road."

"Do you doubt Judge Powell?"

"I am not sure about anything until I see it," I said.

"You are getting to be like James!" Father said.

Then he laughed. "James has gone to China. We will surprise that young doubter! We will have the road when he returns."

At the end of winter, work began on the road. Shaking his head, Father watched the big grader. He did not like what he saw. The grader was making the road level. But it was leaving no ditches at each side for water to go when it rained.

A heavy rain came. The road had never before been so bad. It was completely flooded.

Now we could not use the wagon. We could not walk on the road. We could not ride a mule on it.

Judge Powell said: "Give us enough time, Mick."

"Time!" Father said. "You need a man who knows how to build a road. There was a 17-year-old boy driving that machine."

"He is from the Right Party, Mick," the judge said. "He will soon learn."

"Let him learn on some other road," Father said. His face was red with anger.

When James came home, he tried to walk on the road. But he could not. He came across the hills. His clothes were covered with mud. There was blood on his face, where tree branches had scratched him.

"What happened to the road, Dad?" he asked.

"They sent men who did not know how to build a road," Father said. "But we will get the road. I have their promise."

"You have no more than a promise," James said laughing.

"Wait two months," Father said. "I trust Toodle Powell. He is a great man."

The road builders did not return the next month.

There were small lakes in the road. They never dried. We went two more times to talk to Judge Toodle Powell. He promised again that we would have our road soon.

Another month passed. The road could not be used.

Now Father went once every week to talk to Judge Toodle Powell. The grader came again, with two men. They worked two days. When they finished, the road was like it had been, before the grader came the first time.

Half a year passed.

We went again to see Judge Toodle Powell. "I have bad news for you," he said. "We have no money for roads."

I offered to pay for the stone for our road.

"No one else has offered to pay," Judge Powell said. "That is not necessary."

"You would think it was necessary, Judge," Father said, "if you lived where we live. You live in town. You have a hard road in front of your door. You forget about living where the road can't be used in the winter. We can't all live in town and be judges!"

Toodle Powell's face was red. But it was not as red as Father's.

I knew that it was time to go. "I have work to do," I told Father.

"No need to hurry, boys," Judge Powell said. "Next year we will build you a good road. Remember that your road is not an important road."

"It is an important road to us," Father said.

"And Mick," Judge Powell said, "I want to ask you to help with some work for the Right Party." He tried to keep the happy smile on his face.

Father and I left in a hurry.

"There were small lakes in the road."
Photo by Earl Palmer.

"...he wanted to go to that mountain top."
Photo by Earl Palmer.

Chapter 12

My Father's Wisdom

"Come with me, Jesse," my father said. "I want to show you something you have not seen for many years!"

"It is very hot," I said. "Should you do much walking?"

I did not want to go with him. It was very hot. I knew that a short time ago my father had talked about his health with eight doctors. One had told him not to walk as much as a city block. He told my father to take a taxi home.

But my father had walked home. He had walked five miles across the mountain. Another doctor had told him the same thing 40 years before. He had worked as much as any man in those 40 years and raised a family of five. When he decided to do something, he did it.

I wiped the sweat from my face, and followed him. "Where are we going?" I asked.

He pointed toward a mountain top covered with

trees.

"How do we get there?" I could not see a trail or path.

I followed him across a bridge that he had made. It was one log. He had cut down a tree so that it fell across the stream. The doctor had told him that he should not use an ax. But he wanted to go to that mountain top.

I followed him under the tall trees. We had come here when I was a little boy. We had come here to hunt. That had been almost 30 years ago.

In those days I needed to run when I was following my father. But time had slowed him.

"I like these trees, Jesse," my father said. "Remember when we came here to hunt? Those were good days! That is why I remember this mountain."

"Is that what you wanted to show me?"

"Oh, no, no," he said. He went further up the mountain.

Until three years before, I had been on this mountain top many times. I had never seen anything different or special on this high land. I had seen the beauty of many wild flowers, a few great rocks, and many fine trees.

Now, at the top of the mountain, the trees had been cut down. There was a fence around this ground. "Who did this?" I asked. "Why is it fenced?"

"I did it," he said.

"But why? We have good land in the valley."

"But this land is the best, son!" He lifted some of the soil to his nose. "Like fresh air," he said. "It is pleasant to touch, too."

"But, Dad—"

"I know what you think," he said. "Your mother thinks the same. Why come to a mountain top to plant seeds? But, Jesse, anything that grows in new ground has a better taste."

"I do not see a weed," I said laughing. "Won't they grow here?"

"I won't let them," he said. "This is what I wanted you to see!"

"And you did this after your doctor told you to stop working!"

"Which doctor?" he asked, laughing.

We sat down on a log.

"Twenty times," he said, "a doctor has told me not to work. He has told me to enjoy my last few days. And now I am 70 years old. A man does not expect to live more than 70 years."

"And, Jesse, I will tell you something else. Your mother and I worked on the side of this mountain when we were young. Those were the good days. The land here on the mountain top is like that land on the mountainside, when we began to work there. It was new then, and it was good."

I remembered when my mother and father farmed this mountainside. I remembered when my father made me a little wooden plow. I was six years old. They had brought me here to the cornfield.

And now tall trees grew on the mountainside.

"And, Jesse," my father said, "the doctors told me to sit still. I could not do it. I needed to work. This is real land. I needed to return to it."

From the mountain top, I looked far over the hills where my father and mother had worked. They had cut the trees and planted corn and tobacco. Now my father had returned here and cut the trees and made his last, small garden patch.

I followed him down the mountain.

One morning seven years ago, my father came to my house. He asked my daughter Jane to go with him to a far field. He said that he planned to clean the water holes there for the cows.

Jane was delighted to go.

The field was more than a mile away. The day was beginning to be hot. Jane and her grandfather walked away talking and laughing. He had a hoe across his shoulder. They carried something to eat and drink. She had a small book to write in.

The sun had set when Jane returned. Her grandfather hurried away. He always had work to do.

"Daddy, come here," Jane said. "I want to ask you something."

She was sitting with her small book open. She had filled twenty or more pages with writing. I knew that my father had not cleaned many water holes that day. I knew what he had been doing. He had been teaching Jane.

"Daddy, what tree does this come from?" Jane asked. She showed me a leaf.

Without seeing the tree, I did not know.

"It is from a red-oak tree," Jane said. Then she laughed because I did not know. "Granddad said that you had often helped him cut red-oaks. But he told me that you would not remember. And he laughed."

Neither my father nor my mother ever saw a book about wild flowers, plants, or trees. My father never went to school. My mother went to school for only two years. But these Kentucky hills were their books. They read the earth as children read a school book.

Before we children went to school, we knew almost every tree and flower. We could name them if we saw any part of them.

My father and mother did not agree about much. They did not agree about the Right Party, or the

Church, or friends. But they always agreed on two things: both wanted school for their children and both loved the earth and everything that grows on it.

From my father, I learned how to keep good land for the future. Rainwater can wash away the good top soil. My father knew how to stop this. He never let us plow straight down a hill. We always plowed along the hillside. And if the soil did begin to wash away, he knew how to hold it.

My father was wise. He always said that land did not increase, but people did. He said that we must keep our land for the people of the future.

Walking or riding with me in the valley, he often pointed to old fields where the good soil was gone. "I remember when this field produced a hundred bushels of corn to the acre," he said. Or, "I saw tall tobacco grow here." Or, "Wheat grew here as high as my shoulder. And now look!"

He said that it was bad to let fire burn over your land. His father had cut trees, and then burned them. The soil there had been good, but now it was not.

"A man does not need to read about these things," he said. "If his eyes are open, he can see what happens to the land. Buy more land," he often told me. "And keep it for the future."

He always told me that if I had money I should buy land.

"Walking or riding with me in the valley, he often pointed to old fields where the good soil was gone."

This is what I did. I finally owned 1013 acres of hill and valley bottom land.

"This house needs many things," I said to my mother and father one evening. We were sitting in their old home.

"What is wrong with this house?" my father asked.

"The walls have never been straight. And there are other things. I will do what is needed, if you will let me."

"We have lived here 28 years," Father said. "You children grew up here. You liked it then."

My father and mother did not know that the neighbors were talking about their house. My wife and I had made many changes in our house. Neighbors asked why we never made any changes in my parents' house. They all talked about it.

Our home had been used by many people. Many strangers had stayed there for a night. Others had come and lived there. There were always more than our own family in our old house. This old home of ours looked more used than any house I had ever seen.

"I have always been afraid of the upstairs floor," I said. "Some day it will break."

"It shakes a little when your Uncle Jesse goes up there to sleep," Father said. "But he is a big man. He weighs 307 pounds and that is enough to shake any floor."

"Let us think about it," Mother said.

After a few days I returned to see my mother and father. People were talking more. They were saying that Uncle Jesse's foot had broken through the floor.

"Where can we go, if people work on this house, Jesse?" Mother asked.

"Live in this house while I build you a new one," I said. I pointed to a good place that was near. "You can watch while it is being built. You can have everything the way you want it."

"That place is far from the well," my father said.

"But I plan to have water come inside the house," I said.

"That water would not taste as good," my father said.

"My father helped to build this house," my mother said. "He shaped the stones with his hands when he was 75 years old. I do not want to say good-bye to this house."

"Let us think about it," my father said.

It was not long until they decided. The next day my father came to see me. "The old house is good enough for us. It is home to us. Do not build a new house for us."

Then he seemed happy again, and he went home. But I was not happy. The old house was not warm in winter. All the other six houses on the farm were better.

Then I had a new idea.

I told my father and mother that I would build them a house on part of my farm. I would build a good, modern house. They would have a good road during the whole year. They would not be up on a hill. They would live between my sister Sophia's home and my home. It was the best part.

"What will we do with our old house?" my father asked.

"Rent it. Or let it stand empty."

"I do not want to rent it," my father said.

"We like to live here on the hill," my mother said.

"But the house, Mom..."

"Yes, the house, Jesse," Mother said. "It is the only home that is our own. We all helped to build it. And we will continue to live in this house. But we thank you for what you want to do for us."

I stood there and looked at them. Then I looked at the house. This was home to them. My father and mother, facing the winter wind, were as sturdy as the great hills around us.

I knew that while two pieces of wood, a stone, and a window glass remained together, this would be their home.

A short time after that, my father and I were riding in my car to the market to buy more cattle. Looking through the window, he saw the railroad.

"I see my old friends," he said. "I want to stop and talk to them."

I stopped the car and we got out.

"I have worked many days here," he said, smiling. It was true. He began work there in 1917 and he worked until 1940. His pay was two dollars and 84 cents per day.

There were four men that had worked with my father. There were also some new men. I listened to their talk. It was very friendly. I knew that my father would stay all day, if I would stay too. He loved the railroad and he loved the railroad workers.

"I wish I worked there now," he said when we were in the car again. "I am not as sick as the doctors say."

I did not answer. I knew that he was not well. I knew that he was now 72 years old and I knew that he could not work on the railroad now.

How had he been able to work there for 23 years? He had walked ten miles every day. On short winter days, I had seen him leave by starlight and return by starlight. I had seen him go in all kinds of weather.

And now it was good to remember how we watched for his return. All the children and the dog watched. One of us children always saw him first. But our dog could run faster and always met him first.

This day as we returned from the market, he did not talk about our new young cows. He talked about the railroad. The railroad was his first love. The cows were second.

I thought of his days of work on the railroad. I thought of how he walked to his work every workday. He was never late.

I heard him tell my mother once in the morning, while they were eating in the kitchen: "Sal, with the money I get from this job, we can send our children to school. I do not want them to be like I am. I want them to learn to read and write. I want one of them to be a schoolteacher."

Eventually, five of us combined had a total of 24 years of college and taught a total of 44 years.

My father put us through high school, paid for his farm, built a house, and got supplies and clothes for his family with his pay from the railroad job. He always said: "The important thing is not how much money you have, but how you spend it. I cut with every edge of the ax."

Mitchell Stuart encouraged his children to go to school and become teachers. All five succeeded! From left, Glennis, Sophie, James, and Mary.

"He sat down and talked pleasantly about the horses and cows."

Chapter 13

Father Was Not Afraid To Die

On a Monday afternoon in November, 1954, my wife, Naomi, her sister, Nancy, my daughter Jane, and I arrived in W-Hollow. Naomi's father and mother, Nancy's husband, and my father were waiting for us. I was recovering from a heart attack.

Helped by a person at each side, I walked into the house.

Only my father seemed happy. He, too, had heart trouble. Many times he had nearly died. But he had lived. He was proud that I had lived, too.

"You will be all right. Never lose hope!"

"Dad, how are you?" I asked him.

"I have a little pain sometimes," he said. "Do not think of it. I do not."

Father lived with my sister Glennis and her husband, Whitey. Their house was half a mile away. One morning he walked down the valley to see me.

He sat down and talked pleasantly about the horses and cows. He had changed their feeding time from four in the morning to five. "They do not like it," he said. "But Glennis won't get up at four, like your mother. She won't get up until five."

"I agree with Glennis," I said.

"People should get up in the morning," he said. "They should go to bed early at night."

"People change," I said. "Children always do differently from their fathers and mothers."

He got up from his chair and stood beside my bed. "Jesse, since your mother died, I have been saving some money to be used to bury me when I die. I have saved a little at a time. Now I have a thousand dollars."

My mother had died five years before. He received 60 dollars each month from the railroad, because he had been a railroad worker for many years.

"How did you spend the rest of the money?" I asked, laughing.

"There were things I needed. I have paid for some things at the house."

"Glennis and Whitey have enough money," I said. "You should not pay for such things."

"But Glennis and Whitey are young," he said. "I want to help them. I must go now. I will see you tomorrow."

The next morning he came again. And the next morning, and the next. Then he went home and went

Jesse's brother-in-law, Herbert (Whitey) Liles and Jesse's wife, Naomi Deane Stuart.

to bed. I did not see him for nine days.

Every morning, Whitey took my daughter to school in Greenup. Each time he came, I asked about Father.

"He will not stay in bed," Whitey said. "He goes out and talks to the horses and cows. He thinks no one else knows how to feed them."

Then Whitey took Father to the doctor. On their way back home, Father came to see me.

"How are you?" I asked.

"That pain," he said. "It won't stop. How are you?"

"I will soon be able to use my hands again," I said. "I can move my fingers."

"That is good," he said smiling. "I have been lying in bed and thinking about what we will do next summer. We can work together again, as we did before."

I remembered when he had said that I was one of God's oddlings. I thought that he was the oddling now.

"Yes. We will make a garden together," I said. "It will be wonderful to work with you again. But now you should go home and go to bed." His face was very white and his body seemed weak.

"I have decided to stay out of that bed," he said. "If I have to stay in bed, I will die. That is for sure."

In the morning, a few days later, Whitey said:

"Jesse, your father is not well. We went to the doctor yesterday. When we returned, he did not want to stop here. He said: "No. You tell Oddling that now I am more sick than he is."

That afternoon many cars passed on the road near our house. I went to the window and sat there. "Why are these people going and coming?" I asked Naomi. I knew that they were going to my father's house. There was no other house at that end of the road. "I wish I knew how my father is."

"There are always people going to that house," she said.

"They are going very fast," I said. "Why are they hurrying?"

Then I returned to my bed.

In the evening, my father's doctor came to see me.

"How is Dad?" I asked.

"I am going there now," he said. "I stopped to ask you how you are." He sat down beside me.

Soon Naomi and my doctor, Doctor Vidt, walked into the room. He said: "I came to listen to your heart."

Father's doctor said: "I must go now."

"Do not hurry," I said. "But when you see Father, tell him I said that he should stay in bed. Tell him that I said he should be quiet."

He did not answer, but walked through the door.

"Doctor Vidt," I said, "I wish that you would go and see my father. Perhaps you can stop that pain in his heart."

He did not answer, because he was now listening to my heart. Then he said: "Jesse, I am giving you something to help you rest. I want you to keep as relaxed as you can."

He did this, and then he sat down in the chair beside my bed. He talked about my father. I told him that we planned to make a garden together. Then I began to go to sleep.

"Jesse, I have been asked to bring you some bad news," Doctor Vidt said. "Your father died about an hour ago."

"Oh, no, no, no," I said. I turned over with my face on my pillow, shaking as I cried. Hundreds of thoughts passed through my mind. This little, thin, red-faced man was gone. He had never weighed more than 144 or less than 125 pounds. He was five feet and eight inches tall. But his spirit could not be measured.

For me, he had always been part of the world, and it seemed that he would always be part of it, like a mountain. I could not believe that he was gone.

If he had lived six more months, he would have been 75. I never could believe that he had become old. He was one of those men who seem to belong to the place where they live, like a rock, a tree, or a hill.

For a few hours I was asleep. Then in the middle of the night I got up. When Naomi heard me, she got up, too.

"Is Dad dead?" I asked. "Or have I had a bad dream?"

"No, Jesse, it is true," she said. "I will give you something to help you sleep again."

When my sister Glennis and her husband Whitey came to see me, I asked: "How did Dad die?"

"You will be surprised, Jesse," Glennis said. "You won't believe what I tell you. We thought that Dad was afraid to die. But he was not, Jesse. You know that as a nurse in the hospital I have seen many people die. But I never saw one die like Dad."

He said to me that morning: "Glennis, when a man has so much pain that life is no longer a pleasure to him, it is time for him to die. Do you agree?"

"No, Dad, I do not," I told him. "You can't die anytime you want to die."

"I can, Glennis," he said. "This burning in my chest won't stop. I am lonely without Sal. I have been near to dying for years, but I would not die. You tell Old Oddling that we will not make that garden. Tell him that I am going on a long journey to see Sal and my family and my old friends."

Then he asked for Whitey. Whitey came, running. Sophia came, too.

"Whitey," he said, "I have some money in a box. Spend it wisely. Use every dollar for something important." Then he told Whitey to keep his livestock. He told him what the farm needs now.

"This time I am dying," he said.

"We put him in the bed," Whitey said. Then he said: "Sophia, this is the end. I am blind now. I am going." These were his last words. He began smiling. He died with a smile on his face. I never saw anything like it.

Father was taken to Plum Grove, to be buried. On that day, Doctor Vidt came to see me. He gave me something to help me sleep. While I was sleeping he went away, and Naomi and Jane went to the funeral at Plum Grove. Naomi's mother stayed with me.

When Naomi and Jane returned, I was sitting up, waiting for them.

"Naomi, were many people at Plum Grove?" I asked.

"I have never seen anything like it," she said. "Cars were everywhere. There were more people than I have ever before seen at a burial."

"Were there more than when Mom died?" I asked her.

"Yes, many more. Why do you ask, Jesse?"

"Dad was proud because so many came then. He told me that he had made many enemies. Only a few people, he said, would come to see him buried."

"He was not wrong about many things," she said. "But he did not know how many friends he had."

I went to the door and watched the sun setting beyond the Plum Grove Hills. Father had met Mother at the little Plum Grove Church. She was 18 and he was 20. He had married her a year later.

Now they were joined again at Plum Grove, sleeping side by side. They lay near where we children had sat, when the Plum Grove schoolhouse was there.

We gathered flowers and took them to Plum Grove, Naomi was driving the car. Jane held containers of water for the flowers. I held the basket of flowers. We moved slowly on the road, around the side of the hill, down a valley and up another hill.

This was my first trip to Plum Grove since the summer before. This was my first time to see the place where my father and mother lay side by side. Beside them lay my two brothers.

There were stones to mark the place. Plum Grove seemed well cared for. The grass was green. The sky

Plum Grove Cemetery.

was blue, with white clouds. All around, but far away, were the Plum Grove Hills.

It was the best place that I knew to lie down under a cover of soil.

As I looked at the stones, I remembered what my father had told us. Years ago he said to Sophia, Mary, and me, when we walked three miles to the Plum Grove school: "Children, I want you to stay together. Then you can help each other. Jesse, stay near the girls. You must stay together."

My father believed that a family should stay together. Such a family was strong.

There were nine in our family, seven children and the father and mother. Now four were sleeping at Plum Grove. The bodies of my two brothers had been brought here. My father had wanted that done. A year after they were moved, he was brought here to lie beside them.

The family was staying together.

One morning a few months after my father died, I felt my strength returning. I walked up the hill where we had planted corn. Now the forest was covering the hill.

How long, when a man must lie in bed, before the

forest covers his fields again?

Not long!

And before my illness, I had not been working enough on my farm. I had not had enough time.

Now I had time. I was happy to be able to walk again on the farm.

I remembered the world of long ago. I remembered when my father and mother lived and worked here. I remembered Dick and Dinah, the mules, and our dogs. The corn had been gathered. I was writing my first book. I loved Naomi Norris, and I walked across the high hills to see her three times each week. I carried flowers that I gathered as I walked.

I would like to start my life again, do again all that I did when I was young.

After the pain and fear of a heart attack, a person learns that living is very near to dying. He knows how wonderful life is.

I had seen the past. Now I had to turn my face toward the future. The future seemed better, because I was able to walk again.

I knew that these acres belonged to me as my fingers belong to my hand.

I remembered when we cut the trees from this hill, almost 40 years ago. My father, mother, and I, and our little thin mule, Barney, got our food from this soil. The soil was thin. It should not have been used. But

"I loved Naomi Norris."

we learned how to grow corn here. If the weather was good, we had enough to eat.

We gave corn to Barney and to our cows. Barney was part of the family. The cows gave us milk and butter. We liked cold milk, and we liked butter on hot cornbread. Our cows got good corn, because they were important to us.

We used the best corn for next year's seed. The next best corn was for our bread. Cornbread gave us strength. And we needed strength.

Mother, Father, James, Mary, and I worked as a family in our fields. Working together gave us great strength.

No one farms these hills now. I do not know a man who would work as hard as we worked for our food.

Chapter 14

I Think I Hear His Footsteps

I looked for him all day, but I did not see him. It was the time of year he liked to be going about. In April, he was always walking with a seed bucket or a hoe or both. Sometimes he went down the road driving a team, a big black horse and a much larger mare with a straw colored mane and tail. There he would be sitting upon the little seat over the wagon bed with the leather check line in his hands. He was a little man, and he would be sitting there on the creaking wagon with plows, hoes, mattocks, axes, and scythes loaded in the wagon bed.

He never drove or walked past that he did not have from one to a half-dozen dogs following him. Only two were his dogs. But other dogs liked him, and they trotted in front of the big horses or followed the wagon. This small man had a kind voice for horses and dogs. I kept looking for him to drive the horses by, but I did not see him. I often thought I heard his wagon and I would go to the door and look, but it was something else. I heard the wind in the oaks on the hill, the big weeping willow or the wild plum trees.

And sometimes I thought I heard his footsteps going down the road in front of my house. But I did not see him. It was a little trick my mind played on me. I knew he should be coming along at any time. Because he was a part of this valley. He was a great part of it. He came to this valley when he was sixteen years old. And he grew up here. He was a young man before he went outside this county. He was almost sixty before he was a hundred miles from home. He was never happy anywhere but on this little spot of earth. When he was away, he worried until he got home.

He had a daily routine. His horses expected him to be at the barn at four in the morning. His cows expected feed in their mangers at this time. And their patient soft brown eyes lit up, and the horses spoke to him when he reached the barn. His hogs spoke to him from the pen until he fed them, too. They liked breakfast early, before the chickens flew down from the trees to help them eat their corn.

This was the way of life for this little W-Hollow man. For almost three-fourths of a century, he greeted his animals morning, noon, and night, fed them, bedded their stalls, and was kind to them. He loved animals, and they loved him. In the spring of the year, especially in April, he got all his livestock onto the green April grass. He put milk cows in a pasture, his horses in a pasture, mules in another, cattle in others, and he had a small pasture for his hogs. He gave animals range and freedom.

Sometimes, when I thought I heard footsteps on the walk around the house, I would go to the window. I expected to see him walking to my tool shed with a hatchet in his hand. Sometimes he used all his staples or nails, and he would drop by my tool shed to see if I had any. Then, too, he might have needed one of the tools in my shed. They were always there for him. His tools had always been in his tool shed for me. His tool shed was four-tenths of a mile away. I suppose his tools were in order. He had always kept them that way. This was the time of the year I expected him to be coming around to look over the fences to see if the wind had blown a tree across one or if a post had given way. We had miles of fences on this farm and each April he had always gone over each fence, with his hatchet and wire pliers, and staples in his carpenter's apron, carrying along some extra pieces of wire and a pair of wire stretchers and staple pullers. He always went prepared to do a job.

So many times he passed here with a hoe across his shoulder. I knew, when I saw him coming with a hoe, that he was either going to the pasture to clean out the water holes in the spring or he was going to hoe one of his many garden patches. He had gardens all over this farm, from the valley to the top of the highest hill. He planted potatoes on high hilltops in new ground to grow them good and big if the season had plenty of rain. And just to be sure, he planted some in the old land down in the bottoms, where, if the season was dry, he'd still have potatoes. He raised tomatoes in new ground so they would be soft and have a sweet taste. He set them in old ground to be sure of a crop. He planted corn, peas, beans, carrots, beets, and lettuce this way, too. He was the best gardener we had in W-Hollow in my day and time, and he was always getting better. He studied land, plants, and seasons each year. He always wanted to learn more.

I saw a ditch yesterday on his land when I walked up the hollow to look at his pasture hill where he and I cleared the ground a long time ago. Now the cattle have so often walked in a single file down the hill to the stream to get water that they have made a path, and water has flowed down the path and erosion has started. I wondered why he had not been there with some of last year's corn fodder and laid it in this ditch. Or why he had not cut sprouts and put their tips uphill to catch the wash of the next rain and stop erosion. That is the way he taught everybody around here, his

"... he taught everybody around here, his sons and others in W-Hollow..."

sons and others in W-Hollow who came to his farm. He never let a ditch start. He could not stand to see a scar on his earth.

And he would not let anybody hack one of his trees with a hatchet, or ax. He would not let any boy carry a BB gun over his ground to shoot at his wild songbirds. He followed the stream through his farm to see if it was choked and had broken from its channel. If it had gathered sticks, brush, or small trees into a dam, he cleared it out and let the backed-up water flow away. There was not anything on the ground, in the streams, among his trees, up in the air, he did not watch. He was the most alert man I ever knew. A fire could be two miles away and he could smell leaves burning and would come running with a hoe over his shoulder and be at the fire before anybody else. He always went first. He always got the jump on anything before it got the jump on him. He got control of weeds when they were small. He cut his corn before frost. He dug his sweet potatoes before frost bit in the vines. He dug his Irish potatoes before the autumn rains.

He was the first man ever to try new grass seeds on the W-Hollow hills. He was the first man to try to get a road built up the valley. He split blighted Chestnut trees for bridge flooring (because he was not able to buy flooring sawed by the mill) and built eight bridges so we could get a road. He was the first in this rural area to have electricity, for he had the first Delco system at his house. He was the first man to have a registered bull. He kept a registered bull for thirty years and charged only a small fee for his services to improve livestock here. I saw his young bull, a registered Polled Hereford, when I walked up the valley yesterday. It seemed that this sun-and-wind-tanned little man without a trace of gray hair on his temples should be standing beside his stocky, curly-haired Hereford bull rubbing its shoulders and neck. But he was not there. It was terrifying not to see him.

I walked on up the valley to his barn. I could almost feel his presence there. In the mornings he always cleaned the stalls and rebedded them. Over there was his sweet-potato bed. Below it was his garden. This time of year I should be able to hear his laughter. It always rode on the W-Hollow April winds. Or he might be out somewhere in a patch of dogwoods, for they are in bloom now. He always liked them. He always liked to find a dogwood beside a stream where he could look at the white blooms and hear the water run at the same time. But I did not see him beside the dogwoods up that way, and I did not see him beside the stream.

It was not unusual for me to be looking for him. This entire valley was his beat. Exactly how many people have lived in this valley of W-Hollow since 1900 I do not know. But of all of them, not a one could have known more trees, wild flowers, cliffs, squirrel dens, hawk's and crow's nests, and groundhog and fox dens than my father. No one knew where more wild strawberries grew, more hickory trees that bore nuts, more black and white walnuts, than Mitchell Stuart.

No man had ever plowed more miles of furrow than he. He must have plowed enough land for a single furrow to reach around the world. Men have said that his plowpoint had hitched on more rocks and roots than any other man's. Old men and young said his long-handled goose-neck hoe had turned over more gravel from year to year on every square foot of available W-Hollow farming land than had the hoes of any two other men. He knew this land. It was his land. It possessed him, and he possessed it. He was a part of this land, and it was a part of him.

Why do I keep looking for him? Why doesn't he come? Why do I think I hear him and his team go past when it is only the wind in the weeping willows and in the oaks on the hill above his house? Why do I hear him on my walks? Why isn't he here?

He must be here. He could not leave this valley. He could not get away from it. Especially not now, while W-Hollow is an array of wild flowers on every bluff. In April, when all the blooms are out, this is the most beautiful valley in the world! The small W-Hollow man kept fires out of W-Hollow, so wild flowers could grow and bloom and young timber could grow up sound as silver dollars. Only one fire ever reached his acres, and lightning set it. But he got that one out even though it was set in three places at the same time.

Knowing he is dead and buried, I still find it hard to believe he is gone. This is why I hear him when it is only the wind in the willow leaves. I think I hear his hoe turning the stones over again in his corn row. How can he leave this world where his image is stamped upon everything? He is still a part of this valley.

Prayer For My Father

Be with him, Time, extend his stay some longer,
He fights to live more than oaks fight to grow;
Be with him, Time, and make his body stronger
And give his heart more strength to make blood flow.
He's cheated Death for forty years and more
To walk upon the crust of earth he's known;
Give him more years before you close the door.
Be kind to him – his better days were sown
With pick and shovel deep in dark coal mine
And laying railroad steel to earn us bread
To carry home upon his back to nine.
Be with him, Time, delay the hour of dread.
Give him the extra time you have to spare
To plod upon his little mountain farm;
He'll love some leisure days without a care
Before Death takes him gently by the arm.

Jesse Stuart

Her Work Is Done

I thought my mother was a forceful river
When as a child I walked along beside;
I thought that life for her would be forever,
That she would give me counsel, be my guide.
She gave me counsel as the years went by;
She taught me how to use a heavy hoe
On mountain slopes that shouldered to the sky
In stalwart corn and long tobacco row . . .
And as I grew in strength to meet the years,
Among the clouds, up with the mountain wind
She would not have me bow to petty fears,
She taught me courage that was hard to bend . . .
Now time has passed with many seasons flown
On mountain slopes my mother's work is done;
That forceful stream that was my mother's own
Flowed quietly toward the set of sun.

Jesse Stuart